His hands tangled in the hair at the nape of her neck, and with a yank, he forced her to raise her chin.

She had been kissed. But those clumsy fumblings had held nothing like this. No unerring aim to invade her mouth with the flavor of excitement; no warmth from his lips to heat her own, carrying fire all the way to her toes; no increasing tenderness to make the sound of his quickened breathing a melody to her ears.

Christina melted toward him. Her eyelids drifted closed, and she offered herself most willingly to the nibbles he trailed down her neck. . . .

By Patricia Wynn
Published by Fawcett Books:

THE BUMBLEBROTH
A COUNTRY AFFAIR
THE CHRISTMAS SPIRIT
A PAIR OF ROGUES

A PAIR OF ROGUES

Patricia Wynn

FAWCETT CREST • NEW YORK

A Fawcett Crest Book
Published by Ballantine Books
Copyright © 1997 by Patricia Wynn Ricks

http://www.randomhouse.com

Library of Congress Catalog Card Number: 97-90280

ISBN 0-449-22815-0

Manufactured in the United States of America

First Edition: September 1997

10   9   8   7   6   5   4   3   2   1

In memory of my kind, gentle mother-in-law
Dorothy Davis Ricks
April 9, 1912, to December 25, 1996

Chapter One

*H*er Grace, the Duchess of Broughton, gazed adoringly down at her baby in his cradle. His little cheeks had taken on the soft, rosy color of a peach, and the fuzz upon his head had the silky texture of down. Cushioned, as he was, in a profusion of lace-edged pillows and snowy linens, and weighing only slightly more than ten pounds, he seemed rather small to be a marquess; but every time his mother looked at him, she felt the deep maternal pang of love.

Her husband, the duke, came up behind her and put his arms about her waist.

"Isn't he perfect?" Louisa whispered, her cheek pressed closely to his.

"Perfect," Robert agreed. His voice grew husky. "I can hardly wait to make another just like him."

As his hands began to rove, Louisa turned and threw her arms about his neck. "Oh, Robert!"

Moments later, she emerged from their embrace with her body atremble.

"We've been so blissful." The heavy sigh accompanying this statement alerted her husband to the probability that something of a devious nature was in her mind. "Isn't it a shame that everyone cannot be as happy as we?"

Robert, who by now knew his clever wife well, asked warily, "Whom precisely did you have in mind?"

Louisa sighed wistfully again, and he suppressed an indulgent laugh.

"I was thinking of Ned," she said. "Ned and Christina."

The first name so startled Robert, he gave an incredulous jerk. "Ned? As in Windermere? You can't be serious."

"Of course I am, my love."

Robert groaned. "Now, Louisa, you cannot possibly be thinking of finding Ned a wife?"

"And why not?"

"Why not?" Robert began to lift his hands, then dropped them helplessly at his sides. He spluttered, "Because Ned's a scoundrel, that's why!"

Louisa stared at him, hurt filling her eyes. "You shouldn't say that. Not when Ned is your very best friend."

"My very best?" Robert gaped. "I've never called him anything of the sort."

"But you asked him to stand godfather to our precious Robert Edward!"

"Louisa . . ." Exasperation wrinkled Robert's brow. "That was *your* idea, not mine."

"Oh . . . well . . ." Louisa waved that inconvenient fact away. "Well, perhaps it was. But you agreed! And just look at the good that has resulted. Ned has called to see his godson every day since you asked, and I'm certain he is drinking less."

This was true, and Robert was willing to concede the point. Though fond of Ned, in a rather theoretical way, Robert had resisted Louisa's suggestion that the Earl of Windermere be asked to act as patron to their baby. He had no desire to run the risk of having his son influenced by one of the most notorious rakes in all of Britain.

Secretly, too, Robert had dreaded the prospect of broaching such a tender subject with one whose devilish humor discouraged any sort of serious discourse. But Ned's reaction to Robert's proposal had surprised him.

When asked to stand as sponsor to his lordship, the Marquess of Drayton, Ned had been so taken off guard that for once the sardonic grin had been completely wiped from his lips. A curious glow had flickered in his eyes, momentarily replacing the satirical glint that always seemed to linger there. He had accepted the honor gravely, then with an immediate reversion to his usual manner had proposed toast after toast to the young marquess until Robert had perforce called a halt.

"But, Louisa," Robert resumed his argument, "even if Ned has his better moments, I still cannot conceive of a girl who would be suitable for a man of his reputation."

"I was thinking of Christina."

"Christina who?"

Louisa stared at him as if he had suddenly lost his mind. "Why, your sister, of course! Have you forgotten her altogether?"

"My sister!" Now Robert was truly aghast. "You mean to say that I should marry my own flesh and blood to a man of Ned's repute?"

"Yes. Don't you think they would suit?"

"Suit!" Clapping one hand to his forehead, Robert paused in horrified contemplation. "They would suit a great deal too well, if you only knew. Mixing Christina with Ned would be like throwing lard upon a fire."

"What a horrid way to talk about your sister! Lard, indeed!"

"Now, Louisa, you know perfectly well I am not referring to Christina's figure. It couldn't be more elegant." Robert grimaced, as if his words had raised a dreadful thought. "If I know Ned, he will find it all too alluring."

"There, then." Louisa gave her husband a smug little smile. "What could be more perfect? Christina will be arriving tomorrow for the christening. We need only bring them together and see how they get on."

"No." Robert spoke with all the authority a duke could muster. "I simply shall not allow it, Louisa. Christina is enough of a handful as it is. Why do you think my mother sent her to that ladies' seminary for all those years?"

He paused before adding, as if the words had been wrung from his mouth, "There have been reports from the school. I did not tell you because I did not wish to shock you, but there was something about Christina and the dancing-master and a dare . . ." Robert took a harried breath. "Suffice it to say that she does not need a husband, or even an admirer, who remotely resembles Ned. What she needs is a good, stodgy fellow, someone dependable who will keep her in line."

"How dreadfully dull. But that is an excellent tack to take, my love. If you set yourself against them, Christina and Ned are sure to be safely wed by August."

"Louisa . . ."

As if sensing his father's mounting frustration, Lord Robert Edward awoke to emit a ragged squall.

His Grace refused to debate the issue further. In a huff, he left the nursery, determined to think the subject closed.

That evening before dinner, he was taken by surprise when Louisa raised it again, this time in front of Ned.

The future godfather had come to dine and to make his daily visit of inspection. The baby and his cradle had been carried down from the nursery, so that his parents and their guest could have the pleasure of the little marquess's company before their evening meal. Ned, who was clothed in a snug-fitting coat that matched the black of his hair, had just bent over his tiny lordship's bed to scoop him up in one strong hand.

"There now, Little Ned," the earl said, settling the

bundle on his forearm. His dark brows rose as he studied the sleeping baby. "Let me tell you about the adventures Uncle Ned has in store for you."

"The boy is to be called Robert," said Robert. "*Not* Little Ned."

"Whatever you say, Bobby boy, but I thought it the godfather's duty to name the child. And should I get nervous in church—which I might, considering how many years it's been since I've set foot in one—I might omit the name Robert entirely."

Robert grinned. "You wouldn't dare. And it's no use, Ned. You can't bait me the way you used to."

"No?" Ned sighed and shook his head. "Another of life's little pleasures gone. I suppose it is Louisa's fault. What I must have been thinking when I encouraged you to pursue her—although I never had marriage in mind, you know, but something of a more lascivious nature."

Robert was on the verge of making an angry retort, when Louisa swept into the drawing room.

"Quarreling again?" She searched her husband's face before directing him a reproachful look. "You mustn't let Ned tease you, Robert." She strolled to Ned's side and reached for her son. "Isn't he a dearest? Come here, little one."

Robert's temper waned as he watched his friend carefully hand her the swaddled bundle. Against the flame of Louisa's red hair, Ned's darker locks gleamed like the devil's own coal, but for a brief instant, the hard planes of his face had softened in greeting.

Not that a respite so short could erase the signs of dissipation from Ned's face. At one time, Robert recalled, Ned had been accounted a vastly handsome man, but his skin had grown too dark and rough to grace a drawing room and his reputation was much too soiled.

But Ned was responding to Louisa's question, and

his impertinent words drove all other thoughts from Robert's mind.

"My godchild is a rare work of art, perfection itself." To Robert, he added sotto voce, "Good work, Your Grace. I'm glad you finally took my advice. Didn't know you had it in you."

"Ned—" Exasperation raised a flush on Robert's face. "I would remind you that my wife is present."

Ned widened his eyes, the very picture of innocence. "But, Bobby boy, surely Louisa knows how the baby was conceived?"

"That's enough . . . ," Robert warned.

"You mustn't let Ned tease you, my dear." Louisa smiled calmly at them both, as she swayed side to side, embracing their infant. "He is simply trying to conceal the fact that he envies you."

A patch of crimson appeared on each of Ned's cheeks. "Touché, Louisa. She is right, you know, Robert." A rare note of sincerity had crept into his voice. "If all God's mites were like this one, I should not mind having one myself." The cynical gleam reappeared in his eyes. "But then, who knows? Perhaps I have a number already."

At Louisa's cry of admonishment, he added unrepentantly, "I was just about to tell Robert Edward about the delights I have in store for him when he gets older—say, in about thirteen years."

"Were you?" Louisa said, with a show of unconcern. "In that case, I shall tell you about the plan I have for you."

"What plan?"

"Louisa . . ." Robert had glimpsed the purposeful spark in her eye. He knew his beloved wife. She took on projects. Many kinds of projects. And it seemed she had decided to make the Earl of Windermere her next.

"Robert and I—"

"Absolve me please, Ned," Robert interjected. "I had nothing at all to do with this."

"*Robert and I* have been thinking it is long past time you were married, Ned. You would make a wonderful father."

Ned stared. "You are jesting, surely."

"No, I'm not."

"But, my dear girl. Who would have me? Who would *I* have, if it comes to that?"

"There must be someone, Ned."

"Not necessarily." He paused and then smiled knowingly. "I get it. You are worried about my succession, but you needn't concern yourself, you know. I have a cousin somewhere or other. Undoubtedly, he will make a much better earl than I."

"I am not worried about your succession," Louisa enunciated clearly. "Although I daresay you could do much better by your estate. And if you took the trouble to build it up, you would have some wonderful funds to spare for my societies. But—I can see by your sour expression that that particular notion does not appeal to you."

"It does not," Ned agreed. "I will have you know that I did not come here to be abused or mistreated—or solicited for more subscriptions. I came to see my godson, to ensure that he was being properly raised. But if this is what poor Little Ned has to look forward to . . ." He shook his head in mock despair.

"I told you, Louisa"—Robert chuckled at her ruffled sigh—"you've lit upon the wrong man. Better to drop the notion."

"Well . . . we shall see." Louisa raised her nose in the air. "But if the perfect girl were to happen to come along—"

"No!" Robert knew exactly what she had been about to

say, and just *whom* she had been about to mention. He did not want even the seed of Louisa's notion to be planted in Ned's fertile brain. But he could see out the corner of his eye that his vehemence had been a serious tactical error.

"But wait. My dear Robert . . ." Ned hadn't failed to sense his agitation and was quick to take advantage of the chance to annoy him. "Why do I get the distinct impression there is something you are trying to conceal?"

"It is nothing." In spite of his efforts to appear unconcerned, Robert knew his words sounded curt.

With a sigh, Louisa put on a wistful expression. "It is certainly nothing now. I *had* come up with who I thought would be the perfect match for you, but Robert says he is entirely opposed."

"Is he now?" Ned's brows rose. The glint in his eyes was more pronounced. "And who might this paragon be?"

"I am afraid that Robert has forbidden me to mention her name," Louisa said.

"Now, wait!" Robert felt at a loss. He knew what she was up to: She was trying to make Ned curious. Nothing like forbidden fruit to entice a rake. "There is no secret about it," Robert said, purposely nonchalant. "It was quite simply a silly idea, and so I told her. Ned will agree."

"Shall I?" Ned asked slyly. "Then why are you so flustered, Bobby boy?"

"I am not flustered—or if I am, it is because I do not like to discuss my sister in such an outrageous way!"

"Your sister, is it?" Folding his arms across his chest, Ned leaned back against the chimneypiece. Comprehension flooded his face. Comprehension . . . and a flicker of some bleaker emotion. If Robert hadn't known his friend far too well, he would have called it hurt.

"Your little sister, I take it. What was her name—Catherine?"

"No, Christina," Louisa said. "She's a delightful girl—spirited, beautiful. I thought she would be just right for you. But"—she sighed dramatically again—"it is not to be."

"But, after all, why not? Surely Robert couldn't object to my meeting his sister?" Ned made an evil face.

"Why wouldn't I," Robert retorted, "when I had second thoughts about your meeting my wife?"

In the ensuing silence, Ned went very still.

"Robert!" Louisa rushed to intervene. "What a terrible thing to say! And you know it is quite untrue. You could not wait to present me to Ned."

Deeply chagrined, Robert was relieved to see an easing in Ned's stance. He had not meant to wound his boyhood friend. He wouldn't have thought it possible in any case, if he had not just witnessed the change in Ned's expression.

But the devil would goad him!

Robert tossed a sheepish grin to his wife, grateful for her diplomacy. "I couldn't wait to show you off, that was all."

"And who better to show her to, eh Broughton, than the man who made all your happiness possible?" Ned had quickly recovered his sangfroid. "Louisa, I am not at all certain if you realize how instrumental I was in bringing about your wedded bliss. Why, if I hadn't coaxed Robert and taught him everything I know—step by lurid step—he might never have gone as far as to hold your hand."

He turned toward Robert. "You did at least hold her hand, didn't you, Broughton?"

Robert had to grin, though at times he could happily throttle Ned. Louisa was blushing—and so charmingly,

Robert wanted to rush her upstairs right now. But that was to be expected around Ned. One could not be in his presence long without one's thoughts being led astray.

"That is as may be," Robert said, clearing his throat, "but my sister is entirely another matter. She's an innocent, Ned, and she'd bore you to death within a sennight."

Ned felt, rather than heard, the seriousness beneath Robert's banter. He ignored the resulting pang and waved Robert's words aside. "No need to worry," he told him. "If I make any villainous plans with respect to your sister, I promise to keep you informed. I pride myself on my transparent nature."

Robert grimaced. "How you comfort me. But I daresay Christina can take care of herself." He gave a startled sideways glance, as if he'd let slip something he shouldn't. "Not that she is anything but innocent, mind you. She is just out of school. Quite young, you know. Not your usual type."

"Sounds terribly dull," Ned reassured him.

"Indeed. After the christening, we plan to bring her out. Louisa has offered, and my mother has agreed. Mama is too old, she says, for the rigors of London."

Ned nodded, and his voice went glum. "Almack's. Court presentations. I shudder at the thought."

"I knew you wouldn't be interested."

At the sound of Robert's relief, Ned couldn't resist another barb. "But, my dear fellow, if the chit's your sister, how could I not be intrigued? You must add me to her list of swains. I shall grovel at her feet."

But he had missed his mark. Robert merely laughed. "I'd love to see you grovel. I'd love to see you die for a woman's sighs."

"Not bloody like—Oh, pardon me, Louisa! Yourself excluded, of course. I was all prepared to grovel, but Robert threatened me bodily with a sword."

"That's very sweet of you, Ned." Louisa gave him a motherly smile before cocking her head at the sound issuing from the hall. "That is the dinner gong. Robert, would you take the baby while I ring for Nurse?"

Ned watched his friend cross the room to take his son from his wife, and an unfamiliar weight settled on his chest. They made such a pretty picture—mother, father, and child. And an unusual one at that.

Dukes did not generally cradle their own offspring. Neither did duchesses for that matter. But Louisa refused to be bound by the rules that constrained them all.

And Robert was happy because of her. God knew, as did Ned, that Robert's upbringing had not been an affectionate one. No more than his own, Ned reflected bitterly. Eton at six. The cold indifference of schoolmasters. No protection from sadistic senior boys for whom one had to fag. The early separation from parents, who had no particular interest in one, anyway.

And yet, here was Robert, thoroughly domesticated. He had two adoring spaniels at his feet, and was billing and cooing over his little marquess like any nursery maid.

And—if he could only see himself—he was eyeing Louisa as if he could hardly restrain himself until time to go to bed.

The emptiness of his own life pressed heavily on Ned. Damn, but he was envious! However, he promptly reminded himself that a rake had no business even thinking of marriage. No decent girl would consider marrying a man of his reputation. And he had had enough of the other kind to last him a lifetime.

With the baby asleep in his arms, Robert preceded them from the room, meeting the nurse in the hall. Louisa accepted Ned's arm.

"Robert is right, you know," Ned said to her in a

confidential tone as they strolled toward the dining parlor. "I would make the very devil of a husband."

"I think you are sadly mistaken. We would so very much like to see you happy. And I cannot help feeling that the perfect match is awaiting you just around the corner."

Ned chuckled in response, but his laughter was forced. "I wasn't made for such things, my dear. My life has been a dismal trail of debauchery and seduction." He tried to lighten his tone. "Besides, I know you are wrong, because the hair on the back of my neck is lying flat."

Louisa paused, holding him back. "I beg your pardon?"

"Didn't Robert tell you?"

Louisa shook her head.

"I have the most extraordinary gift. When marriage is in the air, the hair on the back of my neck always rises, like a dog's when it senses a threat. It comes in quite handy, I assure you. It's got me out of a sticky spot or two."

This wasn't true, of course, but it was his usual tale designed to entertain his hostesses, and Ned almost believed it now. "I felt it quite strongly when you and Robert were courting," he said. "Wagered a hundred pounds at White's on the outcome of your affair and made a nice, tidy bundle when you married. Paid off my immediate debts and carried myself for months on the surplus."

Louisa dimpled as they resumed walking. "And you say you've felt nothing of the sort since I mentioned Christina?"

"Nary a twinge."

But the strange thing was, Ned felt a frisson right now, just at the sound of her name.

Louisa's smirk must have had something to do with it. She looked as if she knew something he did not, and the result was that the hair on the scruff of his neck was bristling. He hid a shiver.

Lousia watched him closely. "You're certain you feel nothing at all?"

"Positively not."

"That is just as well, I suppose." As she swept toward her place at the table, however, Louisa managed to look uncommonly delighted. "For, as he said, Robert is quite opposed to the idea."

As Ned pushed her chair in, she glanced back at him with a secretive smile. "Quite *adamantly* opposed."

"Christina!"

As Lady Christina Lindsay descended from the carriage that had carried her up from Bath, she spied a redheaded whirlwind descending from the steps of Broughton House. Louisa embraced her, then gave the coachman his instructions, before drawing Christina quickly into the house.

Christina decided, as she did every time she saw her new sister-in-law, however brief their visits tended to be, that she liked Louisa very much. She had not been certain what sort of reception to expect when she had been foisted upon Louisa by a mother who could not be bothered to come to London herself. The Dowager Duchess of Broughton had made it clear that her family should expect no more of her efforts on their behalf. Her husband's death, she said, which had occurred a year before Robert's marriage, had robbed her of all desire to live.

From Christina's perspective, the Dowager did not appear to have altered at all.

Her mother's normal failings were only half the reason for Christina's nervousness today. By now, she was certain her sister-in-law must have been made aware of her damaged reputation. Her own mother had declared her a rag-mannered hoyden since birth.

Why would Louisa want the trouble of bringing out such a girl?

But whatever secret fears Christina had harbored about her reception were momentarily laid to rest by Louisa's warm welcome.

"I shall give you five minutes to examine your room, and then you must come see Robert Edward."

"See the baby?"

"Yes, of course. You will love him. He is so droll."

Christina laughed. "Louisa, you must be the only mother in London to say such a thing about her baby. Would you not rather relate to me the horrors of your lying-in?"

"Pooh!" Louisa dismissed these with a toss of her carrot-colored locks. "I can assure you they are easily forgotten. I quite ignored them myself as soon as I saw my darling."

Bustled up to her room, Christina could only marvel again at this strange creature her brother had wed. Who ever would have expected somber Robert to have so much sense? Twelve years younger than he, Christina had only sketchy memories of her serious elder brother. Seeing him with Louisa the first time had been a startling experience. The air between them had seemed to vibrate with a curious kind of energy. It had been something she could not fathom, but had vaguely envied.

After a quick freshening-up, she joined Louisa in the nursery. With conspiratorial smiles, both ladies tiptoed over to the cradle. Robert Edward was fast asleep. Their presence must have disturbed his little lordship, for he yawned and stretched with his tiny eyes still closed, poking out his swaddled bottom until his back arched at an impossibly concave angle.

Christina gave a low, watery laugh and promptly fell in love.

"I'm so happy you invited me to be his godmother," she whispered, as she and Louisa retreated from the room.

"I knew you would love him. You are just like Ned."

"Ned?"

"Yes. The Earl of Windermere." Louisa closed the door to the nursery and led the way back downstairs. "He is to be godfather."

"Godfather—Ned?" A vivid memory flooded Christina's mind: a head of windswept hair, as thick and black as pitch; a pair of merry eyes with a teasing gleam; two strong arms; and a comforting lap.

She waited until her sister-in-law and she were safely ensconced in Louisa's withdrawing room with the doors firmly closed, before saying, "The rake? I thought he and Robert had parted company many years ago. It is certain in any case that I've heard of Lord Windermere's tainted reputation, even so far away as Bath. He doesn't seem to be the sort of man Robert would have for a friend."

"Ned has his moments," Louisa admitted, "but he has been so good to Robert and me. And he adores the baby."

His handsome face flashed before Christina's eyes again. "He always did like children," she said.

Louisa paused in her stitching. "I didn't know you two had ever met."

Christina grinned. "You could scarcely call it a meeting. I doubt if he remembers me at all. I was five and he was seventeen. He came down with Robert on the long vacation, but had the good sense never to come to Broughton Abbey again. Of course, I doubt my mother would have allowed Robert to invite him again."

"Oh, dear." Louisa seemed strangely discomposed. "What did he do?"

"I've never been entirely sure." Christina frowned, searching her memory for clues. "Something to do with the upstairs chambermaid, as I recall. It wouldn't have

15

taken much to turn our mother against him. She's referred to him ever since as 'that horrid Windermere boy.' "

"Yes, I believe that is precisely how she referred to him in her last letter. I'm afraid I was so unwise as to advise her that we had chosen him for a godparent, but she *did* ask. Still, I shall refrain from asking Robert about the incident, and I would advise you not to either. Their friendship always has a rather . . . precarious feel.

"But what about you? You were very young when he came. Why do you remember him?"

A smile pulled at the corners of Christina's mouth. "I remember him as the only one of Robert's friends who ever made me sick."

"Not sick!" Louisa looked stunned—and strangely disappointed.

"Not in the way you think," Christina said, laughing. "I meant quite literally sick. I was playing out in the park with my nurse, when Robert and he passed by on their way to hunt. When Ned saw me, he ran over and grasped me by the wrists. He started to spin me about in a circle faster and faster. I was rather frightened at first, and then delighted by the ride."

She made a disparaging face. "I suppose I must have giggled too much, for as soon as he stopped I began to feel ill. I'm afraid I lost my breakfast all over his boots."

Louisa covered her mouth with one hand. "Oh, dear. He must have been quite put off. But what did the boys do? Were they horridly callous?"

"Not at all. Ned was very contrite. He held me on his lap until my spasms passed. As I recall, Robert stood around and looked helpless."

As soon as she'd felt better, her brother had consigned her to Nurse's care, but not before Ned had kissed her on the cheek and said he was sorry. He had given her a hug and dusted off her dress before she was led away. Nurse had scolded, of course.

Christina emerged from her memory to find Louisa gazing at her speculatively.

"Perhaps that was the incident that angered your mother."

"Oh, no. We made a pact of secrecy before Nurse carried me off. I never told on him, and I'm certain that Robert never did. Nurse would not have wished to either, or she would have been blamed for letting me play with the boys."

"I hope you haven't nourished a disgust for Ned all these years," Louisa said on a questioning note.

"Of course not." Christina chuckled. "I should think he would be the one to have a disgust of me." If he did not, he would be one of the rare ones. She had managed to offend most people with her antics. Gazing at her sister-in-law now, Christina wondered how long it would be before she managed to offend Louisa's sense of propriety, as well.

"I don't think Ned recalls the incident."

Christina knew a moment of disappointment. "No, of course he would not. Why should he remember a little girl he met just once?"

Louisa sighed. "Yes, men are so insensitive. They never cherish romantic moments."

"Romantic? Louisa, you cannot be serious."

Even Lousia laughed. "Well, perhaps not. Perhaps you and Ned were never meant to be a couple. I can see that now."

"A couple?" Christina felt a curious fluttering in her stomach. "What on earth are you saying?"

"Oh, I must not mention it," Louisa said, rising from her couch. "Just a silly notion of mine. But dear Robert is entirely opposed."

"Opposed to what?"

Louisa's smile faded. She breathed a heavy sigh. "You will think me quite silly, considering what you have just related, but knowing you both, I had thought . . . I had just briefly hoped that you and Ned might make a match."

"How absurd." Christina felt the feebleness of her response.

"Isn't it?"

"Of course it is. Why should you hope for such a thing?"

Her eyes downcast, Louisa fingered the skirt of her dress. "It's Ned. I know he's lonely. He may seem like a rogue, and I do not doubt he gets up to the worst possible mischief, but I do think he would make a wonderful husband for some fortunate girl. And you seem so alike in the way you both took to the baby. And of course, it would be lovely to have him in the family. . . ."

Louisa was rambling, and Christina knew she should stop her, but an image of Ned's handsome face had come again into her mind. She had never forgotten that face: his big, dark, laughing eyes, with their hint of secret delights. They had swum before her vision many times, almost as if he were twirling her still.

She gave her head a mental shake and said, "You are being fanciful."

"Yes, and so Ned told me."

"Ned told you. . . ." Christina felt color rushing to her cheeks. "You never had this conversation with Ned!"

"Well, not this precise one, I don't believe."

Christina burst into a laugh. "Louisa, you are outrageous. The poor man. You will be quite fortunate if he even shows up at Westminster Abbey tomorrow. I expect he will avoid me like the plague."

"It is just as well." Louisa shook her head despairingly. "As I told you, Robert would not hear of it at all. In fact, he would much prefer that Ned not meet you. He does not trust him."

"Indeed." Christina could feel her hackles rising. How dare Robert concern himself with whom she should meet!

She was no longer a schoolroom miss. She had been restrained long enough—at her school, sometimes forcibly when her rebellious nature had led her to commit unpardonable acts. Coming to London was supposed to mean freedom, and, she had hoped, a blessed end to her unrelenting restlessness. She'd be damned if she would allow Robert to dictate her taste in men!

But she had learned one thing, at least, at that dismal seminary. She gave Louisa her most earnest look and said, "I would never want to do anything to disappoint you or Robert."

To her astonishment, the smile Louisa gave her was full of a cryptic satisfaction.

"That's quite all right," Louisa said. "I am certain you will not disappoint me."

Chapter Two

"Dearly beloved, ye have brought this Child here to be baptized. . . ."

Yes, we have, Ned thought. *And received a rare tongue-lashing for it.* The previous prayers had been designed to make men such as he squirm in their pews, dwelling as they did upon the sins and omissions of everyone present. *Except for little Miss Debutante.* Ned stared across the baptismal font at Robert's sister and scowled.

He had remembered her as a taking child, with long, silky hair and big, wondrous eyes full of trust. Her hair now was only slightly less blond than before, but it had been schooled into sleek obedience. Her eyes were demure and downcast as an elegant female's should be. Though her figure was undoubtedly tempting under that fur-trimmed pelisse, nothing she wore had been designed to attract a gentleman's attention. In short, she was the perfect debutante, fresh out of school and ripe for the Marriage Mart.

The Lady Christina Lindsay should have come as no surprise. Robert had said she would be as tedious as all the other girls her age. Still, Ned had held a glimmer of hope that her trusting eyes would still hold a touch of their childish wonder. Instead, they seemed to look on the world with the same elegant disdain displayed by all the Lindsays.

With her willowy figure and skin like an English rose—and even without her considerable fortune—she should have no trouble snaring some poor duke or earl. She'd make the perfect centerpiece for his home, the treasured ornament of his hearth, as long as he didn't mind being bored to death.

Ned thought of Louisa's suggestion that he and Christina should suit and almost snorted aloud. Nothing about this chit could tempt him. And the notion that Robert would allow him within fifty feet of such a model of deportment was twice as ludicrous.

She was far too virtuous for him and he too ruined to touch her. As he flinched under the archbishop's prayers, the contrast between them made him increasingly irritable. She was standing in the transept with perfect composure, looking for all the world as if butter would not melt in her mouth.

At least the hair on the back of his neck had recognized its error. It lay as unruffled against his skin as a dead mackerel on the beach.

"Dost thou, therefore, in the name of this Child, renounce the devil and all his works, the vain pomp and glory of the world, with all covetous desires . . ."

Ned winced.

". . . and the sinful desires of the flesh, so that thou wilt not follow nor be led by them?"

He panicked. *Renounce them for myself or for Little Ned?* He wished he had thought to ask for a clarification. He was quite willing to renounce them on Robert Edward's behalf, but did he have to give them up himself?

Suddenly conscious that both Louisa and Robert had turned to stare worriedly at him, he quickly found his place in the prayer book.

"I renounce them all; and by God's help . . ."

Little Miss Debutante took up the words when he did. She must have started to say them earlier and had to wait for him. Ned counted himself fortunate that Robert wasn't close enough to kick him. He certainly looked as if he wanted to.

Startled into awareness by the uncustomary pause in the liturgy, Christina realized that everyone was waiting for her to speak her part. She hastened to locate the proper response and began reading with Ned.

She had been dozing with her eyes fully open. Having been forced to attend daily prayer for so many years, she had become quite adept at appearing attentive when her mind was otherwise employed. The archbishop's low, monotonous voice had been just the thing to induce mesmerism in one so deeply ingrained in these habits.

She cast a glance Ned's way and thought he looked a bit paler than he had at first sight this morning. The disappointment she had felt on seeing him still festered in her breast.

Gone was the fun-loving boy she so clearly remembered. In his place, she had found a jaded rake. He was handsome, of course—if anything, more devilishly handsome than before. His years in Town had given him a polish that only a complete Corinthian could acquire. His morning coat of blue superfine, his snug buff trousers, and his striped waistcoat fit his lithesome figure like a glove. His ebony hair, cropped fashionably short, had not one single lock out of place.

Seeing him outside the abbey with his air of arrogant ennui, Christina had felt an urgent need to tuck her unruly wisps of hair beneath her hat, but then her temper had been aroused. When presented to her, Ned had made her his deepest bow, a sure sign of irony. He had looked her over with a lecherous gleam undoubtedly intended to frighten away young damsels on the catch. As if she had designs on him!

Certainly, he seemed to have no memory of the day he had held her on his lap.

The boyish laughter was completely gone from his eyes. In its place, all that remained was a cynical glint. No warmth. Nothing but a harsh self-regard.

". . . then also on thy part take heed that this Child learn the Creed, the Lord's Prayer, and the Ten Commandments, and all other things . . ."

Christina saw Ned's eyes grow round, and she stifled a giggle. For a hardened rake, these would be onerous pledges indeed. She doubted he would make the slightest effort to keep them.

But no matter, she thought, gazing over at Robert Edward. With her for a godmother, he needed no one else, least of all a selfish rogue like the Earl of Windermere.

"I will by God's help."

Ned sounded as if he needed some powerful help right now.

Ned had begun to perspire. If he had known the herculean burden this office would be, he might never have accepted the honor that had been thrust upon him. He'd had no idea that godfatherhood meant anything. He could not remember who his own godparents were—or, for that matter, if he had any. But now that he knew Little Ned, there could be no turning back. The boy was clearly going to need him. With Miss Prim-and-Proper for a patroness, the child had to have someone looking out for his back.

"Grant that he may have power and strength to have victory, and to triumph, against the devil, the world, and the flesh."

"Amen," Ned said loudly. He felt he could drink to that, if a drink were available.

"Lift up your hearts."

Surprisingly, Ned's heart did feel a gentle lift. There was nothing like a fresh challenge to get one going, no matter how great the sacrifice. Still, he would have to consult with an authority to see precisely how far these damned oaths were meant to apply to his own conduct.

The archbishop had moved to take Robert Edward from Louisa. The boy was all done up in white satin and lace. Ned would never have believed how sweet a boy could look in such a rig-out.

Then, before Ned's thoughts could drift any farther in that pleasant direction, Lord Robert Edward began to howl.

Ned gave a start, but he stopped himself just in time from reaching for the boy.

The archbishop seemed to feel there was no cause for alarm. He went right on with the service, ignoring the fact that the Most Honourable the Marquess of Drayton's screams were growing louder. And louder.

Little Ned doesn't like to be held that way, you dolt.

Ned barely managed to contain his temper. Louisa and Robert were turning pale. Even Miss Perfect had begun to look wan.

Bet they don't have noises like that at her select ladies' seminary, Ned thought with a painful wince. *Let's hurry up and get this over.*

"Name this Child."

At last they had come to the good part.

"Robert Edward Charles." As he said the boy's given names, Ned's chest filled with pride, which was spoiled only slightly by the knowledge that he had to share the honor with Little Miss Perfect.

Oh, well. The chit was certain to marry in short order, and then he would have Little Ned to himself.

"Robert Edward Charles, I baptize thee In the Name of the Father, and of the Son, and of the Holy Ghost. Amen."

Relieved at what appeared to be the end, Ned heaved a sigh, but his relief was cut short when the archbishop started up again. "We receive this Child . . ."

The service went on and on, but now it was accompanied by the baby's shrill cries. Ned felt his nerves begin to shatter. Heat and chill coursed through his veins. He had to stand pinned to the abbey floor while Little Ned grew so red he bordered on the purple. Ned wondered how Louisa could bear to allow this terrible torture to go on.

Four more prayers. Then five.

One had to hand it to Little Ned. Wellington himself could not have battled for so long.

"Grant that you be strengthened with might by His Spirit in the inner man . . ."

The boy had strength enough already. No diminishment of tears no matter how many prayers he had to endure.

Ned felt exhausted, though, as if he had drunk for days on end and wrung out his insides. Then the archbishop said "amen" again, and Louisa rushed to take her baby. Robert Edward's shrieks turned quickly to gasping sobs. A blessed sigh issued from both godparents.

Ned glanced Christina's way and saw how stricken she appeared. Gone was the English bloom from the rose; she looked almost green.

What right did she have to turn green over Little Ned? Poor boy. It wasn't his fault.

"Shall I take him for you?" Ned asked Louisa. "You

must be exhausted." His hands fairly itched to hold the baby.

"No, thank you, Ned." Louisa appeared to be slowly recovering. The baby's sobs had turned into hiccups. They could all go home.

Ned felt the need for strong drink. He would head straight for his club and douse his shaken feelings, and hope his nerves would recover one day.

"You could do one thing for us, however," Louisa said. "Robert and I must go directly to call on my uncle and aunt. They will want to hear right away how the baptism went. We would be very grateful if you could entertain Christina. Perhaps a drive around the park?"

Louisa flashed him an innocent smile.

But Ned could not be fooled. He grinned back, doing nothing to hide the irony in his response.

"Of course, my dear. I would be delighted to show young Lady Christina around. Robert, I presume you have no objections?"

But Robert was absently frowning. It was easy to see he had been unnerved by his baby's cries. He looked as if *he* needed a bracer, but the poor old fellow had to brave the family instead.

Ned decided to take pity on him. No sense in teasing the fellow after all; this was Louisa's scheme.

"Uncle Ned will take good care of her, never fear." He offered Christina his arm and patted her hand in an avuncular manner. "Come along, then, Lady Chris."

Uncle Ned?

Christina could barely contain her indignation as she accepted Ned's escort from the abbey. She did not like to take orders. She chafed under pretense. But more than anything, she abhorred condescension.

In her gaol-like school, however, she had learned to hide a full range of emotions. She smiled sweetly up at

Ned and was her most demure as he handed her into his waiting carriage.

They drove to the park in silence. Christina folded her hands in her lap like the veriest schoolgirl, determined to bore the very dickens out of Ned. She was tempted to exclaim over the sights to emphasize her naïveté, but in her frazzled state, she was not sure she could achieve the proper note. She was still unsettled by the baby's cries. If she had been Louisa, she would have snatched him from the priest, archbishop or no.

"What a perfect day for a drive." Ned's words, issued in a sarcastic drawl, broke into her musings. "Thoughtful of Louisa to suggest it."

The day was anything but perfect, as Christina could see. Still in the midst of winter, the trees stood lifeless and bare. A bone-chilling breeze was gusting off the Thames, making her shiver in spite of the woolen rugs piled high on her lap.

Christina was agreed that Louisa's subterfuge had not been very subtle, and she thought it as futile as Ned obviously believed it to be. Determined, however, not to show that she had detected his irony, she replied demurely, "Yes, my lord."

"Are you quite warm?"

"Yes, my lord."

"Was your journey to London pleasant?"

"Yes, my lord."

Ned cocked a dark look her way. "You're a prodigiously agreeable chit, an't ye?"

"I try to be, my lord."

Her sickly sweetish tone drew a suspicious glance from him, but after studying her profile to no effect, Ned shrugged and chirruped to his horses.

They were a beautiful team, Christina noticed as they swept into the park: two well-muscled bays with a smooth, long stride and strong, arched necks. Confident of her knowledge of horseflesh, Christina could see that Ned had chosen them for their gait rather than for show. Matched grays would have been more fashionable, but this pair performed as if they had been stitched together at the shoulder.

"You have a fine pair of horses, my lord," she could not keep herself from saying.

"Indeed I do."

"May I drive them?" If he ever saw her skill, it would put a stop to his condescension.

A garbled sound came from Ned, and for a moment she thought he might choke on shock.

"No, Lady Chris," he finally managed. "I very much regret that you may not."

"Why?"

"Because you are a girl, and these are my bays. You couldn't handle them if you tried."

"Is that so?" With an effort, Christina struggled to keep the innocence in her tone. "I am accounted to be something of a whip, my lord."

"By whom?"

"By my groom."

Ned's lips turned up smugly at the corners. "One's servants are not always the most impartial of judges, as I am sure you will agree, my dear."

Christina fumed, but, eyes downcast, she made a timid reply, "I am sure you are right, my lord."

Ned drove on, but Christina seethed with offense. That made two slights now, two intolerable insults that she needed to avenge. *Uncle Ned, indeed!*

Never behindhand when the occasion called for revenge, she searched about for the first opportunity.

Despite the cold weather, the park was not totally devoid of company this morning. Here and there, she spied a gentleman exercising his mount. Surely one of them could be useful in a pinch if she could only think of a way to punish Ned for his insufferable arrogance.

Ned had reached the end of the row, and now he turned his horses into the wind. Through stinging eyelids, Christina scanned the park. The turf was gray and lifeless, but so wide and open, she quickly formed an idea.

As Ned gave his bays more rein, she surreptitiously reached into her reticule and pulled out a handkerchief. Before he could glance her way, she discreetly dropped it by her side.

The wind caught the linen and blew it backward, but even so, Christina waited until they had traveled a pace before sounding the alarm.

"Oh, my!"

"What is it?" Ned turned with a start.

"I am afraid I have lost my handkerchief." Christina craned her neck as if to search behind them and put one hand to her lips. "Oh, dear. I do believe it is way back there."

"No matter. I am certain you have another."

Christina scowled. She might have known he'd be no gallant. "But I am afraid I don't. At least, not like this one." She sniffed. "My dearest grandmama—God rest her soul—embroidered it for me. I am quite attached to it."

Ned frowned and gave her a look of disbelief. "You're attached to a handkerchief?"

Christina nodded. She had a gift of making her eyes turn red at the rims. She used it now. It was one of the advantages of being blond. With this cold wind blowing on her face, however, she imagined they looked quite pitiful already.

"Oh, yes," she said with a sigh. "It is utterly irreplaceable. If you could just fetch it for me, I would wait for you right here. I should be most grateful."

Ned cleared his throat in a disgruntled manner. He brought his horses to a stop and turned to glance around. Against the bleak landscape, the handkerchief was scarcely more than a white speck in the distance.

"I shall certainly not leave you here. We shall turn and go back."

Christina kept the sweet smile pasted on her lips even while worrying that Ned's plan would spoil her own. If he could scoop the kerchief up without bothering to descend from the carriage, then she would have to come up with a different manner of revenge.

She ought to have called out sooner, she thought, but of course, she had expected him to stop immediately as any gentleman should. She ought to have known he would act the scoundrel.

They retraced their steps at a spanking pace. Ned was leaning to the outside, lining up his horses with the kerchief so he could bring them to a halt at precisely the right spot. Christina could see that such a feat would be easy to one who drove so well. She thought of distracting him to spoil his aim but was sure he would simply back the bays until he was right again.

Disappointed, but not defeated, she watched him guide the team to a perfect stop. He was leaning down for the kerchief, when a sudden gust whipped it from his grasp and carried it off into a ditch.

Ned muttered curses under his breath.

Christina felt like cheering inside, but pulled her lips into a pout. "Oh, dear. Oh, dear. What a shame!"

Ned's brows contracted in a look of disbelief.

For the briefest moment, Christina worried that she might have overplayed her empty-headed role. Schooling her features into a more credible expression, she offered, "I shall hold the reins for you while you fetch it."

Ned hesitated, eyeing his bays with reluctance.

She added, "Surely you can trust me to do that much." She gave him a wistful smile.

Sighing, Ned made a sign for her to hold out her hands. He took the reins and wrapped them properly through her gloved fingers.

"Hold them steady," he warned her. "They're a bit frisky because of the weather. And make no sounds to them, mind."

Christina nodded, the very image of the dutiful schoolgirl.

Ned glanced at her uneasily before leaping to the ground. Something about her struck him as suspicious. It was hard to believe that anyone, even a girl fresh out of school, could talk like such a ninny. But he could not refuse to retrieve her property, nor could he make her fetch it herself.

The kerchief was only a few steps away, but in a depression, too low to reach from his carriage box. A fresh gust chilled the back of his neck. The wind was turning brutal. As he reached down for the handkerchief, he cursed it and Louisa's scheme for dragging him out to the park.

Just behind him, he heard a brisk "chirrup!" A slap of the reins made him pivot in time to see his horses bolting.

"Hey!"

He took off at a run, but the bays outdistanced him. Christina was leaning forward in the box, looking for all the world as if she were urging them on.

Ned glanced quickly about. Two men were cantering toward him. He ran to stand in front of them and motioned for them to stop.

"What the devil—"

Recognizing one of the men, Ned shouted to him, "Levington, your horse!"

"Is that you, Windermere? What's toward?" Startled, the other man's horse began to dance.

Ned evaded its flying hooves. "Hurry man, I've got to catch that girl. She's got my team."

He reached for Levington's reins, but Levington held on to them while he scanned the park. "A girl, is it? I'll stop her for you."

"No!" Ned shouted, but his protest came too late.

Spinning his horse, the dastard escaped Ned's grasp and set off at a gallop after Christina.

"Damn!" Ned turned to the next fellow, a stranger to him. "Sorry, but I am taking your horse."

"The devil you are!"

Ned took no chances this time. He seized the fellow's reins and his jacket and, in one movement, yanked him from his saddle.

As the gentleman hit the ground, an oath issued from him. "You will name your seconds, sir!"

"Very happy to oblige"—Ned leapt into the saddle and spurred the stranger's horse—"as soon as I throttle that imp."

Surprisingly, Christina seemed to have come to no harm yet. She had somehow managed to turn his bays before they dashed into the street. Hundreds of yards in front of him, she was rolling along the lane, the reins still gripped between her fingers, her body relaxed. The carriage was turning in a wide circle. At a suspiciously steady pace.

Levington had nearly caught up with her. With that head start, and with her circular path, he had cut across the turf and come to a halt in front of her.

"No, you idiot!" Ned swore to himself. Then, just as he had anticipated, his horses shied from the sudden assault. They swung to the left. Christina made a grab for her seat with both hands, losing the reins in the process.

Now the bays bolted in earnest.

Ned spurred the horse beneath him. In less than a minute he had closed the gap. Keeping clear of his team's line of vision, he came alongside them and grabbed the ribbons before restraining his mount.

The stranger's horse resented this rough treatment. He tried to veer away, but Ned held him steady. With his thighs and forearms taut, his muscles wrenching, he finally dragged his frightened bays to a stop.

"Mercy!" Christina's relieved tone would have made him laugh if he had not been so furious.

"What the devil do you mean by—!"

"Miss, are you quite all right?" Levington galloped up, and his hasty motion set the bays to rearing and kicking again. Ned was nearly jerked off his seat.

"Levington, you ass, stop spooking my horses!" Ned shouted as he settled them down again.

"Why, Uncle Ned! What a thing to say—"

Ned whipped around in shock at this mode of address, just in time to see Christina extend her hand to the other gentleman.

"—when your friend has just saved my life."

"Him?"

Ned's indignant cry was interrupted by Levington, who raised a mocking brow. "*Uncle* Ned? I did not know you had a *niece*, Windermere." His provocative tone revealed that he had much mistaken the situation.

"She is not my niece," Ned said through gritted teeth. He knew very well what Levington had conjectured. Ned would be delighted to strangle Christina, but he could not have Levington mistaking Robert's sister for his ladybird. "She is an old friend, Broughton's sister, the Lady Christina Lindsay." At their expectant looks, he added grudgingly, "Lady Christina, allow me to present Baron Levington."

"Charmed." Levington had the gall to trot his horse closer so that he might kiss her hand, his well-worn manners the epitome of grace.

It was amazing, Ned observed with an angry glance, how well one could hide a bankrupt purse beneath a very little bit of polish.

Christina batted her eyelashes at him. Her hair had escaped from her bonnet. Wisps of blond silk whipped about her face. But even disarranged as she was, with a coquetry Ned had not remarked in her before, she managed to appear suddenly alluring. "I cannot thank you enough for rescuing me, my lord. I am afraid Uncle Ned's horses bolted with me."

"Shame on you, Windermere, for leaving a lady alone with your horses."

"I did not leave her alone, and I doubt they bolted." At Levington's startled frown, Ned decided to drop the subject. "But whatever happened, I need you to return this horse to your companion. I am afraid I offended him."

"What? Grisham?" Levington looked about and spied his friend in the distance, limping toward them. "You shouldn't have done that, Windermere. He is something of a marksman."

"That is marvelous." Ned clenched his jaw, dismounted, and handed the horse's reins to Levington. "He has just asked me to name my seconds."

He turned and climbed to sit beside Christina. "Head him off, will you? I want to get the lady home. Tell him he will hear from me."

"Certainly." Levington tipped his beaver to Christina. "I shall call, if I may, to assure myself that you have recovered from this incident?"

"Please do," Christina said, but her voice was subdued.

Ned glanced her way and saw the guilt in her expression, which confirmed his suspicions.

"Come along, then," he said to her. "Levington, your servant." Ned talked to his horses, and with a gentle touch he coaxed them back onto the road and out of the park.

He decided to walk them back to Broughton House. They had sprinted enough for one day and in their excited state, he could not be certain they wouldn't bolt again in the street.

Christina was silent. After a moment, she said in an abrupt voice, "I am sorry for the trouble I've caused you."

Ned opened his mouth to speak, and his bottled words burst forth. "Well, let me tell you, my girl, that it is not at all the thing to spring your horses—or my horses, or anyone's horses—in the park."

"I wasn't speaking of that. I was speaking of your duel."

Ned was taken aback. "My duel?" He gave a chuckle. "You needn't concern yourself with that."

"But Lord Levington said his friend was a marksman!"

"You didn't think I would meet him, did you?"

Christina's blue eyes opened wide. "But mustn't you?"

He shrugged. "Not if I can help it. I shall send my friend Carnes to speak to him. He's a diplomatic fellow." Ned directed her a chafing glance. "Unless you think Robert would be more suited?"

Christina started up in alarm. "Oh, no, I wouldn't think so! Robert has no experience in such matters. At least, I do not th-think. But what can your friend Carnes say?"

"He will say that I was not myself. That I was sick with dread—because of a lady, you understand—so that I must have lost my head."

"Which, of course, you did not."

A hint of pique lay behind her words. Her contrariness confused him.

"I am certain I would have if I'd been given time to think. But I was angry, you know. I told you not to stir up my bays."

"I know."

Her chin was in the air. It seemed no further apology would be forthcoming. Ned felt his anger resurge.

"So why did you do it?"

"Do what?"

"Don't play the innocent with me. Why did you spring my horses?"

Christina turned round eyes upon him. "Oh, but I didn't. I was sitting there, doing what I had been told, when your nasty horses bolted with me, *Uncle Ned*."

Again that appellation astonished him. "Who gave you leave to call me Uncle Ned? I'm not your uncle, my girl."

"And I am not your girl."

They had reached Broughton House, Ned realized. In his preoccupation, he had guided his horses there without thinking.

"Wait a moment." He grasped her arm as she started to jump down unassisted. "I have not finished."

The chit had thrown him off balance, but he would get to the bottom of this incident.

"Oh?" She turned toward him coolly, and her gaze raked his grasp.

"I asked why you presumed upon our relationship." He could not have a girl calling him uncle, especially not a girl with a face and a figure like hers. "I am not so old as that, and you are not so young."

"You do not think so?"

"No, I don't."

36

"Well, if it amuses you to delude yourself—" She gave a little laugh and a shrug.

Ned knew when he was being baited. He baited Robert all the time, but he discovered he did not particularly enjoy being on the other end. "It amuses me not at all," he said, gritting his teeth. "And I asked, *who gave you leave?*"

Christina turned her clear blue eyes up and widened them into a guileless look. "Why, you did, Uncle Ned. Did you not refer to yourself as such when you escorted me from the abbey?"

Ned sat back and glowered. "I didn't mean it that way," he muttered feebly.

Though . . . he supposed he had. He had been feeling rather put out. The service had rattled him, and then Louisa had made her ludicrous suggestion, just when he was so eager for a little brandy to help him recover. "I was referring to myself with respect to Little Ned," he hedged.

"Robert Edward, do you mean? But you are not his uncle either, so how was I to know?" Christina smiled pityingly at him. "*Of course,* you are not his uncle. However, I"—she turned quickly and jumped down before he could stop her—"I *am* his aunt."

Ned's temper flared. "Oh, yes? Well, we shall see about that, my girl."

"Now, Uncle Ned, you are being silly."

With that parting shot, Christina sauntered toward the house.

Ned stared after her in disbelief. What was the chit so riled about? She was not what she seemed.

His horses stamped impatiently. Knowing he must not make them stand, not after the trauma Lady Chris had caused them, Ned gritted his teeth and urged them homeward.

"Silly, was I?" Ned fumed at this image. Then, he recalled his last words, and an angry flush moved up his cheeks. What *had* he meant by *we shall see*?

One of his horses snorted in derision. It had been a foolish thing to say, Ned admitted. What could he do about it, after all? She was Little Ned's aunt. He was not Little Ned's uncle. The only way he could change that situation would be to make her stop being an aunt or to make himself become an uncle, and how he could do that—

The only possible solution crept into his mind.

And the hair on the back of his neck stood on end.

"Oh, no you don't, my girl." Ned shook his head and grimaced tightly. He had caught himself just in time. Better not to let that notion ever enter his brain.

Himself and that spoiled little chit?

Never.

Chapter Three

*O*n entering Broughton House, exhilarated by her victory over the rake, Christina discovered that her brother and sister-in-law had been home for some time.

Louisa was sitting in the drawing room, cradling the baby. Looking up at Christina's entry, she explained that they had arrived at her former guardians' just as her uncle was settling down for his doze. Loath to disturb him, they had left a message with the servants and hastened home to comfort Robert Edward.

"I cannot imagine what caused me to forget my uncle's napping hour," Louisa said, "unless it was my distress over Robert Edward's crying." She hugged the sleeping baby and cooed to him, "That nasty archbishop frightened my darling, didn't he?"

With her eyes firmly fixed on her child, she asked Christina, with an air of nonchalance, "How was your drive, my dear?"

"It was rather brisk for a drive, Louisa."

"Was it?" Louisa glanced up eagerly.

Christina directed her an accusing glare.

Louisa's gaze faltered. "Well, I daresay my thinking was a little bit muddled, as I said. I hope the weather did not spoil your outing?"

"No, of course not. I always love a rugged bounce."

This comment drew a second curious look, but Louisa

must have decided she would be wiser not to probe, for instead she stood and, bringing the baby to Christina, forced him into her arms.

"Would you kindly help me a moment, dear, and hold Robert Edward while I fetch my wrap? The room has taken on a chill."

Alarmed, Christina fumbled with the blanketed bundle. "But couldn't a servant—"

"No, for I am not at all certain where I left it, and besides, I must speak directly to the chef. I will not be a moment."

Relentlessly, Louisa pressed the baby into Christina's hands, which seemed suddenly to have turned into paws. With Louisa's help, and only because she had to, Christina learned to support the baby's wobbly neck. She was certain he would waken and howl in response to this mistreatment, but, exhausted from his morning exertions, the little marquess slept soundly on.

"Now, sit comfortably here, and I shall be back in a trice. If he wakens, you might try singing to him."

"Singing?"

Christina knew a few hymns, though she feared they might offend his lordship by reminding him of his dip in the baptismal font. She prayed very earnestly that Robert Edward would not waken.

She did not want to sit down. After her skirmish with Ned, she had felt like pacing, but Louisa had left her no choice. After a few anxious minutes ticked by, she began to relax. The baby's sweet scent drifted up to her nose and, taking a whiff, she pondered his unfamiliar essence. It was a soothing mixture of sweet milk, gentle soap, and pure, baby innocence. Robert Edward's soft, little body warmed her breast.

Gazing at his downy blond head, his flat, little nose,

and shuttered eyes, which were certain to be blue, she recalled Ned's words in the carriage.

"*Little Ned*. Is that what he calls you? Hah!" she scoffed. Then she had to stifle her chuckle as the baby stirred and frowned.

She hummed nervously to him. Her song seemed to appeal, for he settled right down. Christina's modest success caused her chest to swell with pride. The glow it kindled there seemed to linger. It calmed her restless heart.

"You don't look anything like Ned," she whispered to the baby. "Do you, little man? If you did, you would have black hair and dancing black eyes and a wicked smile I should be tempted to knock right off your face. But you are nothing like that, are you, my angel, and I wouldn't do that to you, would I? No, but I nearly did it to him."

Robert Edward shifted happily in her arms, and this time she found that his movement did not make her nervous. She was quite good at this, she discovered. She must have a special knack for holding babies. She wondered if Ned knew how to hold Robert Edward and soothe him back to sleep, but she was ready to wager he did not. She would show him her talent sometime and make him squirm with envy.

Ned had gentle hands, of course. She had seen that immediately in the way he handled his horses' mouths. His long, strong fingers had practically stroked the reins. Even when he had taken her hand to place them in it, his touch had been firm and gentle.

A memory of his touch made her close her eyes.

The baby warmed her breast.

"Christina!"

Robert burst into the room with two spaniels at his heels. The baby opened his eyes and gave a burp, and

Christina nearly panicked, but she jiggled him briskly and his eyelids drifted shut.

"Did you see that, Robert?" she whispered, gazing at the baby in wonder. "You ought not to make such noise, but did you see? I got him back to sleep."

"What? Oh, yes. Well done." Robert smiled at his offspring, oblivious to the two dogs jumping against his trouser legs.

When one of them managed to claw a tender spot, however, he noticed their bad manners. "Down, Cassius and Brutus! No need for all this jealousy. Out into the corridor, the both of you, now!"

His spaniels brought under control, Robert straightened to face his sister.

"See here, Christina. Louisa tells me you went for a drive with Ned."

Surprised, she replied, "Yes, of course I did. You saw us go."

"No, I did not."

"Robert"—Christina stared at him, thinking he must have lost his wits—"Louisa told us to go. She practically forced me on Ned. He asked for your permission, which you gave."

"Did I?" Robert's brow furrowed. He dragged a quick hand through his hair. "I daresay I might have." He grumbled, "Fool parson. He must have been deaf."

"Robert!" Louisa crossed the threshold just in time to hear this remark. "I have never heard you speak of a man of the cloth in that way. And the archbishop!"

Robert looked reasonably abashed. "But he would go on so, Louisa, and as if poor Little Robert were not screaming to high heaven."

His indignation traveled to the baby, who let out a cry. Christina's stomach knotted, but she held on to him.

"Do you want me to take him?" Louisa moved to her side.

"No," Christina crooned softly and jiggled. "No. Let me try."

"Then rock him slightly. That's it. You see how he loves you?"

The child had quieted. Looking down at his innocent face, Christina realized she had never felt so loved. Errant tears sprang to her eyes. "He does, doesn't he?"

"Yes, of course. It is a wonder how Robert Edward knows his godparents."

"His god—" Christina looked up. "You mean Ned? I mean, Lord Windermere?"

Louisa sighed happily. "Yes. It gives me such pleasure to watch him. He has a special touch with babies."

"Louisa, see here." Robert had remembered his earlier objection. "Christina says you told them to go to the park together."

"I may have suggested it," Louisa admitted, "but perhaps the weather was not quite right for a drive."

"The weather is not the issue," Robert said, raking his hand through his hair again, "though, now you mention it, it makes matters worse."

It seemed he would not be so easily distracted this time.

"Ned is the issue," he said. "I do not think it wise for Christina to be seen in his company."

Louisa dimpled at him. "Now, my darling, what a foolish thing to say! How could she not be seen in his company? They are both Robert Edward's godparents."

"But a drive in the park is something altogether different. If they were seen by anyone, anyone at all, it is certain to be repeated about Town. And Christina has not even been approved for Almack's yet."

At the mere mention of Almack's, Christina felt a sudden weight descending on her chest, which had nothing to do with the baby pressed there. She had heard tales of Almack's: the strict patronesses and—to her way of thinking—the absurd ban on waltzing. Precisely what she needed, she thought wryly. Another set of restrictions.

But Louisa was saying cheerily, "You have nothing to fear there, Robert, as you must know. Of course, Christina will have vouchers, and I shall take her to Almack's myself. Lady Jersey and the Countess de Lieven will be calling here tomorrow afternoon."

Christina smothered a sigh and held the baby tighter. She could say nothing, of course. If Louisa meant to go to the trouble of bringing her out, then Christina must accept the kindness and pretend that the balls at Almack's were the height of her ambition.

But she wagered to herself that Ned had never been forced to attend the dull assemblies. Rakes were never forced.

She would give anything, she realized, to see Ned be made to suffer the insipidity of Almack's.

Robert agreed with his wife, but grudgingly. "I daresay you're right. Almack's should pose no problem, but I will not have Sally Jersey spreading it about that my sister is receiving attentions from Lord Windermere. Nothing could be more prejudicial to her prospects."

Christina bristled, but again she hid her feelings. *Hang my prospects.* She had no fears that a match would not be found for her; the sister of a duke, with a handsome dowry, would always be sought for her money. She might break every rule Society cherished, and still her suitors would flock to the door.

No one would be put off by the fact that she had ridden in an open carriage with Lord Windermere. No one, at least, who would not be put off by her own antics once he had learned of them.

And, besides, Robert acted as if his friend could not be trusted, when Ned had been the perfect gentleman in the park.

Well . . . perhaps not the perfect gentleman, but he had done nothing to risk her reputation. On the contrary, it was he who had cautioned her about her behavior.

A sudden pang of guilt assailed her. If either gentleman they'd seen should start a rumor about her, it would be her fault, not Ned's. But she could not say this to Robert.

The baby's wet nurse came into the room, a plump, rosy-cheeked woman from Yorkshire.

"Does tha' want me to take his little lordship now, Your Grace?" she asked Louisa.

"Yes, Dobbs. Lady Christina will be growing tired. We have imposed upon her long enough."

Christina did not protest, although she wanted to. She missed the comfort of the baby's body as soon as Nurse took him away.

So Ned had held the baby, had he? She tried to imagine such a tiny mite in his strong arms and found the picture made her smile. How would he quiet Little Ned? Would he twirl him round and round as he had done her? Or sing? Somehow, she imagined Ned's lullaby to be naughtier than hers.

But how curious that a rake would take the time to coddle an infant. Perhaps Ned wished he were a father. For the first time in her life, Christina wondered what it would be like to be a mother.

She was expected to marry. Almack's was known as the Marriage Mart. Somehow, she knew she would find any gentleman she met there as weak as an infant's limbs, but try as she might, there would be no avoiding tomorrow's visit from the patronesses.

* * *

If Ned had had the slightest inkling of the company he would encounter at Broughton House the next day, he would have arranged to postpone his visit. But duty called him. Duty as a godfather—for he had forgotten to see whether Little Ned had survived his christening—and duty to his good friend Robert.

He doubted, somehow, that Lady Christina had recounted her adventures in the park with any accuracy. Most assuredly, the little brat would not have confessed to stealing his horses. And it was entirely possible that she had failed to mention to her brother her meeting with Levington.

Despite his appearance, Levington was not the sort of fellow a man would want his sister to know. Ned knew him well. They belonged to the same club, wagered at the same tables, and patronized the same race meetings. They also visited the same gambling hells and called on the same opera dancers. The only difference between them, as far as Ned could see, was that Ned always paid his debts while Levington seldom did. That, and the fact that Ned was not hanging out for a rich wife.

Overnight, Ned had come to the conclusion that Christina, or at least Robert, should be warned to discourage the baron. And while he was at it, Ned thought grudgingly, he might apologize to Christina for his behavior. It was clear that he had somehow offended the chit, although he couldn't imagine how. Why else would she have sprung his horses?

As a peace offering, he had decided to fetch the handkerchief she had dropped and that both had forgotten. For his morning ride, he revisited the park and found it where it had blown into the ditch.

Dismounting, he retrieved it and held it up to see if it had come to any harm. What he discovered then made him curse rapidly aloud.

The kerchief was not damaged. No indeed. It was as free of soil as it was free of embroidery.

Her sainted grandmother, indeed.

Ned rode to Grosvenor Square in a darkening mood. The imp had made a fool out of him on purpose, and he would be damned if she would get away with it.

When he reached the house, Robert's footman showed surprise.

"Good day, your lordship. I—"

"No need to announce me, Perkins. I'll just have a word with the family. In the drawing room, are they?"

"No, your lordship. His Grace and Her Grace have gone out. The Lady Christina is in, but you might prefer—"

Ned swept past him. "Thank you, Perkins, but I know what I am about. The Lady Christina will do very nicely for now."

The footman seemed to be trying to direct him away from the drawing room, since Christina was in there alone. Well, Ned would have a few words with the little brat while Louisa was not there to protect her.

But as soon as he opened the door, Ned saw what a ghastly mistake he'd made. He had always made it a practice to be on good terms with his friends' servants, so that they might warn him of any situation he would wish to avoid. And here were the makings of the most abominable one he could imagine right now, two patronesses of Almack's, sitting together, side by side, on the couch.

Ned cursed himself for not paying more attention to the footman's hints; however, caught by three widening pairs of female eyes, he could do nothing but hide his chagrin and make his leg to the two visitors.

The Countess de Lieven barely contained her dignity in her surprise on seeing him. She raised one limp-fingered hand to be kissed. Sally Jersey made no effort to hide her voracious curiosity. Her gaze traveled back and forth from Christina's face to Ned's, as if she'd discovered a secret worth her weight in gold.

Christina herself made the picture of unblemished girlhood in her white muslin gown, her fair hair let down to her shoulders and confined with a blue satin ribbon. Her cheeks seemed a mite rosier under the ladies' regard, but Ned suspected she might have raised the color herself on purpose.

Ned cursed his ill luck and the fit of arrogance that had made him ignore the footman's cues.

"Ladies." Recovering, Ned made them his most polite bow. "I had not thought to disturb you, but Broughton's servant allowed that he was at home."

A feeble lie—as he saw when Lady Jersey exchanged an amused glance with the countess and said, "How very odd, when the duke departed only a few moments ago, and through that same door."

"Perhaps the servant had been called away from his post," Ned improvised in an attempt to cover his blunder. "However"—he directed an evil glare toward Christina—"as long as I am here, I should discharge my errand. I have retrieved your handkerchief, Lady Christina."

"My handkerchief?" She gave a polite, puzzled smile.

Blast the girl! She had the effrontery to play ignorant, did she?

"Yes. The one your dear grandmama knitted for you. Surely you have not forgotten something to which you were so attached?"

"Attached? To a handkerchief?" The Countess de Lieven looked down her nose. "Is this a jest of yours, Windermere? It seems in rather poor taste."

Lady Jersey laughed and eyed Ned curiously. "Why do I have the feeling that there is more to this tale than meets the eye?"

"No such thing, my lady, I assure you," Ned protested. He hadn't known which question to answer first, but the comment seemed to cover them both. "I have merely retrieved an object the Lady Christina was so careless as to drop in the park. She assured me it was irreplaceable." He let a note of incredulity color his voice.

Christina's lips were quivering rather suspiciously. He could not tell if she was amused or simmering deep in anger, but his own mouth tugged at the corners with her plight.

"*Uncle Ned* was so kind as to drive me to the park yesterday," she explained to her visitors.

His amusement vanished. There was no need to tell these gossipmongers of their drive. They would have it all over Town by nightfall that he was smitten, when of course he was not. And that Uncle Ned business again—

But the gentleman in him would not allow him to retort that Louisa had forced him to escort her young sister-in-law.

"Permit me to return your property to you and go in search of Broughton. Ladies."

He bowed again and tried to escape from the room, but Christina called him back.

"Uncle Ned, these kind ladies have just brought me vouchers for Almack's."

Wincing at the name, Ned restricted his raptures. "How thrilled you must be."

"Yes, and"—Christina gave him her sweetest glance—"I was about to tell them how much you yearned to attend the assemblies."

"Yearned?"

"Yes. Remember how you were saying you had not been to Almack's since you were a young man yourself, and how you would—what was it you said?—do a penance to be able to go?"

Ned choked on a rapid protest before consoling himself with the thought that a rake like him would never be admitted to that holiest of holies. But much to his dismay, both guests seemed eager to overlook his tainted past. His sizable estate and elevated title would always inspire women to attempt his reform.

Lady Jersey exclaimed her delight and assured him of his welcome at the next assembly. The Countess de Lieven majestically inclined her head, the smugness she felt on finally luring him back to the fold apparent in her thin, cold smile.

Ned could think of no way to disclaim Christina's invention. He could not deny what she had said without offending two of the most powerful leaders of Society. If he had only himself to consider, he might have done it without a backward glance, but he could not make Christina out to be the liar she was.

As she, apparently, knew he would not.

He would have to wring the girl's neck soon, before she tripped into a noose and hanged herself.

Lady Jersey questioned him with a speculative gleam in her eye. "Did you plan to accompany Lord Broughton's party, my lord?"

Ned was happy to see that Christina had the grace to flush. She had intended merely to annoy him, not to trap him into being her escort. Clearly she had not envisioned this.

Perhaps she had no wish for his company at all.

Well, if she was merely determined to make him miserable, he could do her the same favor.

"But of course," he said, enjoying Christina's visible discomfiture. "I promised." Then he smiled at her through gritted teeth. "And Uncle Ned never forgets a pledge, my dear." The glance he directed her promised, *I am going to get you for this, you brat.*

Christina saw the implied threat in his eyes, and a curious thrill tripped along her spine. When Ned bowed himself out, she had to stifle a nervous desire to giggle. He had meant to disconcert her with that handkerchief, but she had bested the rogue again. Ned would think twice next time before trying to embarrass her.

Then, however, the thought that he had committed himself to accompany her to Almack's began to worry her. She only hoped he was not too angry. The martial look in his eyes had warned her to watch her flank.

Though her purpose had been otherwise, her maneuvers had resulted in his being forced to become her escort. Surely such conduct had gone beyond the pale.

This latter thought sobered her until her visitors' call came to an end. Christina saw the two ladies to the door, profusely thanking them for their kindness—and even meaning it when she thought of how they had helped her to vex Ned.

But after they left, she found she was too irked with herself over the result of the encounter to sit still for long. She tried to take up some needlework, but the effort proved useless. She wished she had one of her school chums here to laugh her mood off with, the way they had always done after one of her scrapes. The house seemed empty without Louisa, but even if Louisa had been there, Christina could not very well have gloated over how she had hoodwinked Robert's friend.

Besides, Louisa might put a different interpretation on the whole business.

Lowered by this mortifying thought, and still feeling restless, Christina plopped her needlework back into its basket. She needed to talk to someone. Coming to London should have meant constant activity and crushes of company, a continuous stream of pleasure to take her mind off her discontent. But she had not yet been presented. The rounds of balls and soirees would soon begin, and she would be certain to run into old friends with whom to gossip, but meanwhile, she had no one in whom to confide.

The need to do something, to speak to someone, drove her out of the cavernous drawing room. The footman was gone from his post in the hall, or she might have struck up a chat with him. In her life, she had done stranger things to conquer her loneliness. The desperate nature of it sometimes chilled her and made her as fidgety as a wild bird in a cage.

Mounting the stairs, she suddenly thought of someone who could keep her company. He was a perfect listener, too, and had a unique way of soothing her. Cheered by the prospect, she skipped up the stairway to the second floor and tiptoed toward the nursery.

Christina fully expected to find Robert Edward's nurse on duty and was in the process of inventing some excuse for sending her away, when the sound of a gentleman's voice came to her from behind the cracked nursery door. For a moment, she thought he must be her brother, and she wondered how Robert had returned without being heard. Disappointed, she started to retreat. Then, something familiar about the voice held her: its low timbre mixed with a hint of laughter underneath.

Hesitantly, and doubting the evidence of her own ears, she sneaked to the door and opened it wide without a sound.

Ned was there, sitting wedged into an armchair that was much too small for him, with one booted ankle propped loosely on the opposite knee.

Swaddled in blankets, Lord Robert Edward was nestled in the crook of the bent knee, listening to his godfather talk, with the bemused expression of a myopic Oxford scholar. Nurse Dobbs was nowhere in sight.

"What do you suggest I do about it? Eh, Little Ned?" Unaware of Christina behind him, Ned curled his large hand around the baby's small one. "Someone ought to teach that girl a lesson. Don't you agree?"

Christina covered her lips to smother a laugh.

"You thought I was a master. That's because you've seen me with your father." The baby emitted a gurgling sound. "That's right. I can stir Robert from pompous content to a cold fury in less than fifteen seconds. No one bests me with the taunt. The goad, the spur, the thrust— I've mastered them all.

"But this girl—your *aunt*, as she is so fond of reminding me—is good. I'll grant her that. She's quite adept at teasing."

Christina felt an uncomfortable prickle beneath her skin. She might have listened longer, but she was afraid to hear what else he might say.

She turned to go, but a board squeaked beneath her foot.

"Dobbs?" Ned turned.

Before he could catch her sneaking away, Christina abruptly reversed her direction and stepped boldly into the room.

"So," she said, "you have decided to poison Robert Edward's mind against me. Is that it?"

Ned gave a start, obviously disconcerted to have been discovered in such a revealing situation. He made an attempt to cover his embarrassment, leaning back in the small chair to say, "Someone has to look out for the little fellow." His black eyes gleamed at her wickedly. "If I do not tell him, how is he to know that his aunt is a devilish minx?"

"Is that what you've told him?"

"That, and a few other things. Little Ned and I have no secrets. I was about to ask him why his aunt is such an accomplished liar."

53

"I beg your pardon, my lord?" Christina bristled.

But he was shaking his head. "No, you don't. Do not dare pretend to be offended with me, not after the bouncers you told. I was witness to them, remember?"

When Christina could not reply, he said, "Is that what they taught you in that fancy school in Bath?"

"Yes." Christina clenched her teeth to overcome a sudden urge to cry. "They taught me to dissimulate."

"And very well."

"Thank you, my lord."

An uneasy silence fell between them.

When she had recovered, Christina said, "Where is Robert Edward's nurse?"

Ned shrugged and glanced about. "Gone to run an errand, I suppose. She wasn't here when I arrived, so naturally I stayed to make certain the baby was all right."

"Naturally." Christina did not believe him for a moment. To all appearances, Ned had yielded to the same impulse she had. She nodded in a skeptical way. "But if his nurse has been remiss, perhaps we should report her dereliction. Do you not agree?"

Ned shook his head, avoiding her gaze. "Robert Edward was asleep. I'm certain she planned to return before he awoke."

"Still"—Christina was determined to make him admit the truth—"she ought not to have left him when any *rogue* off the street might have crept in to harm him."

Ned grinned at the barb, giving her a sly wink. "But no one could, you see"—he thumped his own chest—"for Uncle Ned is here to protect his godson."

"What a comfort that will be to Louisa," Christina said wryly.

"I'm not sure it would be, but I am afraid I must be going now."

Feeling as if he'd handled this little contretemps fairly

well, Ned transferred the baby to his forearm, cradling Robert Edward's head on his palm. He slowly worked his way out of the chair, grimacing at Christina's obvious amusement.

More cannon fodder for her, he stewed bitterly. He hoped she wouldn't inform Louisa about this episode. He often came up to see the baby. He and Dobbs had a comfortable agreement. Whenever he came to pay Little Ned a visit, she slipped down to the kitchen for a nice cup of tea.

But he did not necessarily want the whole world to know.

If he kept up his bluff, he might still convince Christina that this present occasion was only happenstance.

"Since you've come," he said, meaning to divert her attention, "you can tend to the baby. Here, let me show you how to hold him."

"Show me?" His high-handed manner had provoked her. "I'll have you know that Little Ned likes for me to hold him. I, at least, know better than to handle him like a football."

She tried to take the baby away from him, but Ned held the bundle high up over her head.

"Gently now, gently," he teased her, as she tried reaching first on his right side, then on his left. "No snatching. The baby won't like it." He tsked. "Where are your manners?"

Robert Edward let out a scream, no doubt objecting to being the object of a brawl.

"See what you've done?" Christina cried. "You've upset him!"

"It's nothing. He'll recover." Ned tried to soothe the baby and keep him away from her at the same time.

"Ned, don't be an oaf!"

The note of real distress in her voice touched a chord deep inside him. "Very well. Since you ask so politely, I'll let you comfort him. He likes to be held close."

He laid the swaddled baby in her arms, and Christina cooed, hugging him tightly across her breast and swaying with a rhythm that seemed to come naturally.

The baby's cries abruptly stopped. Robert Edward turned his face into her breast with quick, vicious jerks. He opened his mouth wide, like a mongoose before a snake, and pounced.

His damp little mouth latched firmly onto her bodice. Christina uttered a squeak.

"Well, well," Ned drawled. "At least he knows a woman when he sees one."

He could see her growing redder beneath the soft, marbled skin of her cheeks. A pulse had started at the base of her throat, and she made a choking sound, something between a gasp and a laugh.

Frustrated by the mouthful of muslin, the baby released her to try again. His lunges grew more desperate with every attempt.

"Here. You take him." She tried to force him back into Ned's arms.

He could see she was flustered.

"Oh, no." Ned couldn't help reveling in her distress. Her voice was all atremble. "I wouldn't dream of taking him from you. You are doing so marvelously."

Completely scarlet now, Christina looked up to retort. But she stopped when her eyes met his.

Ned had not sensed his own tension climbing until the shock of her challenging gaze sent a jolt shooting right through him. Exhilaration tingled beneath his flesh, in a way he had not known in years.

And something else he noticed.

Her long, flaxen hair still had the silky shine and the soft, light texture he remembered. Heightened color had brushed her cheeks, giving them the delicate tint of a rose. And, all at once, Christina looked more fragile than he had thought her.

Her breathing had quickened. Her bosom rose and fell against the baby's clinging body.

Who would have thought that a woman could look so ripe with a baby at her breast?

The air between them grew taut as Ned caught a whiff of her perfume. He knew he should pull away, but the devil inside him had been too delighted to see her discomposed. She had made him feel like an ass more than once in the short period he had known her. In the park and again today, entirely unprovoked, she had beaten him at his own game.

Christina was adept at teasing. But for all her grown-up airs, and the tantalizing figure she could not hide, she was still an innocent. Her blush had told him.

He could not resist, just this once, using his advantage.

He lowered his voice to a whisper. "Perhaps there is something *you* could do to help the baby," he said.

A shuddering warmth stole through Christina's body, as his words evoked a shocking image. Still, there was no condescension in Ned's eyes now.

Robert Edward gave a frustrated wail.

Christina ignored Ned's nearness in her pity for the baby. She hugged him closely to her neck, burying her face near his. "It's all right, little one. Poor baby, please don't cry."

"Give me your hand."

"What?" Christina looked up to find that Ned had moved nearer.

"I said . . . give me your hand." His command slid over

her in a low, provocative voice. He took another step closer, so near his breath stirred her hair.

In a daze, Christina extended one hand. . . .

Ned took her palm between his. He held her first finger close to his lips. "The baby wants something to suckle," he said in that same deep murmur. "You can help him, if you will."

"Don't be"—she gasped, then stammered—"d-don't be ridiculous." Her voice ended on a squawk.

For Ned had taken her finger into his mouth. His lips moved slowly over it, making it moist.

Christina's knees had gone weak.

Before she could protest, he released that finger and whispered, "See?" Then he grasped another and held it out before Robert Edward's mouth.

Fooled by the touch against his lips, the little marquess latched onto her finger like a vise. Christina choked on a rapid intake of breath. She had never felt such strength.

Then she heard Ned chuckle, and his amusement called forth a surge of rage that threatened to choke her. She opened her mouth to shriek—

"Time for nursies, is't?" Dobbs's voice broke in, making them jump, as they spun toward the door.

She must have entered the room under cover of the baby's cries, for even Ned had failed to notice her presence.

"Tha should've rung for me, your lordship, like tha always does," Dobbs scolded. "I'm long past done wif m' tea."

Christina caught Ned's disconcerted expression and shot him a look of satisfied vengeance.

Dobbs came to take the baby from her arms. "Tha mustn't try to calm him thysel', your ladyship," she said with a hearty laugh. "It's me he's wantin', and what I've got."

"Shame on you, Dobbs." Ned cocked a teasing eyebrow Christina's way. "You will shock the Lady Christina if you mention such an indelicate subject."

The buxom nurse covered her uneven teeth and fell into a giggling curtsy. "Eh, forgive me, milady. I'm naught but a country girl, for all that."

Christina raised her nose into the air. "It is of no consequence whatsoever," she said, grateful that the baby's cries had stopped.

One whiff of his nurse, and he had let go of Christina's finger, which had not fooled him for long.

Dobbs fumbled with her smock.

Determined not to let herself be flustered again, Christina fought the urge to flee. But her pulse still raced under Ned's regard.

"Lord Windermere was having his little joke," she said loftily. "It is a most deplorable tendency of his."

"Tha doesn' have to tell me naught about his lordship, milady." Dobbs's wink gave Christina the impression that she was all too familiar with Ned.

For some reason, this suggestion nettled her as nothing else had done. When next she spoke, her tone dripped with scorn.

"Ned?" She glanced meaningfully toward the door. "Would you care to leave or do you intend to watch?"

Instead of the guilty start she'd hoped to provoke, she was treated to a wicked grin.

"Although the prospect sounds most enticing, I fear I ought to shove off. Your servant, Lady Chris."

He bowed in his ironic fashion; then, as he stepped past her, he called his good-byes to Little Ned. But the baby was already enjoying his dinner. His noisy slurps could be heard over the pulse in Christina's ears.

"I have to hurry home," Ned told her with a wink. "I've got to decide which of my jackets would best be worn to Almack's. The hostesses there are extremely particular, you know."

Chapter Four

After this unsettling encounter, Christina would have been happy for an hour of reflection in which to plan her revenge on Ned.

But it was not to be. Not long after she had sought her room, the message was carried to her on a salver that another gentleman caller awaited her below. Remembering the man she had met in the park, Christina hastened to freshen her face and went to greet Lord Levington in the drawing room.

There she found him sitting with Louisa, who had returned from her afternoon outing. Louisa had obviously been entertaining the baron with anecdotes about her charitable societies. As Christina passed through the door, she heard her sister-in-law inviting him to subscribe to an almshouse for wayward females.

Lord Levington fumbled for an answer. Then, seeing Christina, he leapt to his feet with a look of unbridled relief. With a pinched face, which was at odds with his smooth deportment, he hastily explained that he had come to inquire whether her misadventure of the previous day had caused her any lingering distress.

Christina made him a curtsy and thanked him prettily again for having come to her assistance. She assured him she was very well.

"Distress?" Louisa looked up from her embroidery. "Was there a mishap in the park?"

Choosing her words with care, Christina gave an abbreviated version of her ride, leaving out the part in which she had sprung Ned's horses. Aware of his potential use to her, she gave Lord Levington more credit for her rescue than he deserved.

Louisa's reaction was overwhelming.

"How very romantic!" she exclaimed, looking back and forth between them with delight. "Just like the stories of knights and fair damsels in distress. I cannot wait to tell Robert all about it."

"Are you perfectly certain that would be wise?" Christina tried to say this tactfully, but Louisa's enthusiasm had taken her aback. "I would not want him to think that Lord Windermere was in any way responsible. Not when they are such good friends."

And not when it had been her fault, and her fault only. And Robert was sure to blame Ned.

Louisa seemed confused by her caution. The baron was trying to maintain an expression of polite disinterest, but Christina had noted the sudden glint in his eyes when he'd heard Louisa's speech.

There could be only one reason for Levington to care whether Louisa related her mishap to Robert or not. And that was if he had a reason for wishing to impress the Duke of Broughton.

Christina had been raised the daughter of a duke. She knew how many people made their livings off the favors a duke could bestow. She wondered what exactly Lord Levington desired and had a sinking feeling she already knew. His lordship's attentions to herself bore the mark of a determined suitor.

He seemed very eager to know how soon he might be honored with the pleasure of soliciting her hand for a dance at an upcoming assembly. Louisa informed him of the voucher Christina had just received for Almack's.

"Shall we see you there tomorrow night?" she asked him with a beatific smile.

"I shall make a point of going." Lord Levington allowed his gaze to rest significantly on Christina.

His call lasted only a very few minutes, but Christina found herself anxious for him to go. She knew him now for a fortune hunter. Young as she was, she'd had experience of his kind. There was an unmistakable gleam of affection in a greedy man's eyes, and it could not be misinterpreted as a reflection of the woman upon whom he gazed.

"Well," Louisa said, once he was gone, "what a charming gentleman! So polite and attentive. He seemed quite smitten with you, Christina dear."

"Did he? I scarcely noticed, but we have not been acquainted for long. I daresay he was merely being polite, as you said."

Louisa smiled at her. "You must find me very obtuse, my love. I said he was polite, but I did not mean to imply that his attentions to you were nothing but charming manners. However, if you do not wish to discuss your admirers with me, I shall refrain from pressing you."

Her speech was uttered with such a remarkable lack of offense that Christina knew her sister-in-law was not angry. She would have chastised herself for having sounded so distant, but the truth was she did not wish for Louisa to make more of Lord Levington's attentions than she herself wished them to be.

"Not at all," she said, giving Louisa her most generous smile. "I simply do not care to encourage an interest I cannot reciprocate."

"No?" Louisa raised her brows. "Well, I shall not push you then, dear, if you cannot find Lord Levington attractive. But it does seem a shame. Especially after such a promising beginning."

Her next smile was full of mischief. "Although I will admit I was a bit put off by his use of so much pomade. There is something so unromantic about a man whose hair appears as if he spent more minutes over it than the lady he is trying to impress. Do you not agree? And I say this, Beau Brummel or no Beau Brummel."

She stood. "But of course, I should never have mentioned such a detraction if he had appealed to you in the least. Whom you choose to favor or not shall be your own decision." She gave Christina a sympathetic smile.

Turning to go, Louisa excused herself on the grounds that she'd like to visit the nursery before dinner. "For I haven't seen my darling baby all afternoon." She was walking toward the door when she paused and threw back over her shoulder, "I do not suppose you have seen Ned today?"

"Ned?" Christina started, as a memory of their last encounter made heat flood her skin. "Whenever would I have seen Lord Windermere?"

"Oh, he often comes by to see the baby," Louisa replied. "Never tell him I know, but he frequently sneaks up to the nursery to spend a private moment with Robert Edward. I find the habit so endearing, don't you?"

"Absolutely adorable," Christina said wryly, as her sister-in-law exited the room.

So, Louisa knew all about Ned's visits to her baby, and she approved. The thought of how mortified Ned would be if he knew he'd been discovered made Christina eager to inform him, until she reflected that Ned would undoubtedly put a stop to his visits if he realized the truth was out. He would have too much regard for his roguish reputation to continue in such a contradictory behavior.

A sense of how cruel such an act on her part would be

made Christina realize she never would use this piece of information against him. And, besides, she could think of no good reason why she should make Ned feel uncomfortable about coming to this house. Robert and Louisa were his dearest friends, after all, and she would not deprive him of their company.

She would simply have to think of some other way to torment him, next time she saw him.

In the morning, Louisa received a note from Ned informing her that Lady Jersey would be gravely disappointed if he did not accompany them to Almack's that evening. Louisa waited until directly before Ned's arrival to tell Robert of the addition to their party.

"Windermere?" Robert's voice had risen an octave, so he cleared his throat before continuing, "You cannot mean that he will go to Almack's with us?"

"I think it was he. I cannot remember numbering another Ned amongst our acquaintance," Louisa replied innocently, as she applied a dusting of powder to her nose.

"Louisa, you are doing it again. You are purposely misunderstanding me when I am being very serious. What will people say if we appear at Almack's with Ned in tow?"

"My darling, you mustn't talk of Ned as if he were a barge."

Robert spoke in a threatening tone, "Louisa . . ."

Unable to distract him, she sighed. "Yes, my dearest, what?"

"You know I cannot countenance even the appearance of Ned's dangling after my sister."

"Yes, you say that, Robert, but I do not agree. However, there can be no changing our plans for this evening at this late hour without offending Ned irreparably.

What's done is done, and we must contrive to put the best possible face on the evening."

"I cannot understand how you could have gone against my wishes like this."

Robert's plaintive tone brought Louisa to her feet. Moving to stand in front of him, she patted his chest and adjusted the fold of his cravat.

"I did not invite him, dear. Sally Jersey took it into her head to suggest this arrangement, and since we would not wish to offend her, I could see no other choice. But we'll take care it does not happen again. I suppose a word in her ear will do the trick."

"Oh, God," Robert said gloomily. "If she suggested such a thing, it can only be because she heard they drove in the park. She has probably been on the lookout for a match for Ned this many years and thinks she's found him one at last."

"Nonsense. Whomever a man Ned's age chooses to marry is no affair of hers."

"But she will make it her affair. All you women do."

"Robert!"

Robert refused to look sheepish when his wife was so clearly the guilty one. The stare he gave her told her so. Louisa just dimpled at him.

For once, her dimples failed to work their spell. Robert grew stiff, before soberly informing her that he would have to have a word with Ned, man to man. "I must warn him off before it is too late."

"Too late for what?"

Her question disconcerted him. "Why, too late to change his course, I suppose. He must understand that I will never give my consent to a match with Christina."

"Oh." As she released him, Louisa looked thoughtful. She turned away and went back to her dressing table as if she did not wish him to see her face.

Her unnatural silence brought him an unsettled feeling. He had the sense he was about to make a serious blunder, and that Louisa knew precisely what it was. Moreover, it seemed she felt guilty for not being honest enough to alert him now.

"What?" he finally asked. "Why shouldn't I speak to Ned?"

She had started at his first words but she quickly recovered. "I was thinking of your friendship. That is all."

"No, I know there is something else. I know you too well, Louisa."

She gave him a stricken look. "It is only that I was so very wrong about Christina and Ned. I do not think they suit at all, and I am so disappointed. From what I can gather, they took a positive aversion to each other on that drive I forced them to make. And, now, to make everything worse, Sally has made Ned furious by imposing upon him so."

"Yes?" Robert's lips turned up involuntarily at this welcome news, but he comforted his wife with a pat on her shoulder. "Never mind, my love. It is all for the best. Your intentions were good, but it would never do."

"I suppose you are right." She sighed, then added with a glimmer of hope, "However, if you did speak to Ned, it is possible you might be able to awaken his interest. You know how mischievous he can be when he wants to be contrary."

"So that's it, is it?" Robert gave a condescending laugh. "No, no, my dear. I'm afraid I am on to your tricks. I shall not speak to Ned at all. It will be much better all around if we allow matters to take their natural course."

Louisa agreed meekly, although a hint of guilt still lingered in her eyes as she watched her husband walk from the room. As soon as the door had closed behind him, she sighed.

"My poor, dearest love," she said, looking after Robert with true regret. "You will get over it," she promised. "And you will see. They will make the happiest couple."

That night at nine o'clock, Ned presented himself in Grosvenor Square, in knee breeches and white cravat, with the detested chapeau bras tucked under one elbow, fully prepared to entertain Robert's displeasure. He was also plagued by some serious considerations of his own.

He had been rather appalled with himself for using his superior experience in intimate matters to intimidate Christina. The justification he had used for his bad behavior, that she had goaded him to it, could not excuse him, and he was determined never to let her prompt him to such an improper act again.

That he had found his own pulse heightened by their intimacy had been sufficient warning. The answering glimmer in her eyes had sounded a muffled alarm. He could not let himself become attracted to an innocent girl, nor let her fancy herself attracted to him—especially Robert's sister, who, all but Louisa seemed agreed, would be ruined by an association with Ned. The fact that she played pranks like a rag-mannered brat did not make her the sort of creature to deserve being ostracized by the best of Society.

These noble considerations, Ned convinced himself, had been inspired by Little Ned's christening. Through foolish jealousy, he had let himself get off on the wrong foot with Lady Christina, but for Little Ned's sake it was time they put away their swords. She had not intended to trap him into this evening, but her teasing had resulted in a misfire. If Ned were not careful it could result in the ruin of her marriage hopes and a rupture with his friend Robert and all that friendship meant.

Consequently, he was determined to assuage Robert's certain fears by pointedly ignoring Christina all evening. It also should put the budding gossip to rest if he spent the whole of the night in the cardroom with the gents.

He was more than a little puzzled, therefore, to find Robert so full of bonhomie. It was not at all what Ned had been led to expect.

Louisa's relatively sober manner caused him an equal degree of unease. The only reason he could see for such an unnatural reversal of roles was that they had decided interference from them would be unnecessary in one case and of no particular benefit in the other.

Meaning that Christina had showed no inclination to fall for his charms.

This startling fact was borne out by Christina's cool greeting. A dismissive inclination of her silk-topped head told Ned she had not forgiven him for making her feel the little innocent she was. And, also, that she had not regarded that moment when their eyes had struck sparks as anything to remark.

Well, that was fine, Ned thought, trying to ignore the wound to his pride as they rode to Almack's, with Robert's hearty chatter the only noise to fill the air.

Christina looked particularly fresh and innocent this evening. The requisite white gown with a simple strand of pearls on her creamy breast enhanced the image of naïveté evoked by her idyllic English fairness. This childlike appeal should have struck Ned as insipid; however, he knew that a fertile, mischievous mind lurked beneath those schoolgirl features. This gave her all the mystery of a slow-moving river with a treacherous current. One could not stand on the bank without wondering how dangerous it would be to plunge in.

They arrived just as the assembly rooms were filling at the top of the long flight of stairs. Ned made certain to lag behind the ladies, using Robert as a shield. With luck, so long as he kept his distance from them, no one would think to associate his arrival with Christina's.

This hope was quickly laid to rest by the murmured talk that followed them up the stairs. His appearance at Almack's after so many years had set the quizzes immediately to whispering. Even Willis, at the bottom of the steps, had taken pains to double-check Ned's voucher to make certain there was no mistake.

Feeling like a pariah, in a way he had not allowed himself to feel in ages, Ned squared his shoulders and glanced about him with distaste. In spite of the exclusivity of this gathering, there were not above five people in the rooms he would care to call his friends, always excepting Robert and Louisa. For the rest, they were a bunch of prigs. Of course, Robert was something of a prig, too, but Ned made an exception for him.

He was about to bow himself out of the scene to go in search of a game of cards, if he could remember the way to the cardroom, when the sight of a certain face moving toward them made him change his mind. Baron Levington, with his sleek brown hair pomaded and curled, hailed their party.

"Your servant, Your Grace." He bowed formally to Robert, who took offense at this impertinence and raised his brows.

Stepping into the breach, Louisa smiled at the baron and extended her hand. "Robert, I forgot to mention Lord Levington's call on us yesterday. It appears that he and Louisa became acquainted in the park."

Robert quickly rounded on Ned, his bonhomie completely erased. "You presented them?" he asked with reproach.

Ned nodded, a stiffness forming in his neck. "I called yesterday in the afternoon to speak to you about that, Robert, but you were not at home."

Robert's scowl told Ned exactly what he thought of his efforts. Before either man could intervene, however, Lord Levington had already solicited Christina's hand for two of the dances and had been graciously accepted, with Louisa, Christina's supposed duenna, looking happily on.

"You will have to pardon us, Levington." Robert broke in upon their conversation, taking his sister firmly by the arm. "I promised Lord Buffington I would present him as soon as we arrived."

As they disappeared through the crowd of silk-clad ladies and waistcoated gents, Ned gave a secret snort. Buffington was exactly the sort of prosy bore he would expect Robert to fancy for a brother-in-law. But he was no match for Christina's wits or for her charm. The thought of such a waste annoyed him. Robert should be looking for a higher match for Christina than a young buffer like Buffington.

Ned became aware that Levington had been watching him with a self-satisfied expression. He couldn't fathom what had given the scoundrel so much pleasure.

"Dangling after the duke's sister, are you?" Levington asked without a hint of worry.

Ned tossed him a scathing glance to show his opinion of such a ridiculous question. "My interest in Lady Christina is purely avuncular. If you have any thoughts in that direction yourself, however, I'd advise you to forget them. There is no possibility that Broughton would ever countenance the match."

"Why not? The lady is possessed of a clear fortune, as I understand. Why should she not follow the dictates of her heart?"

Ned did not like the gleam in Levington's eye as he dusted his sleeve with a small pinch of snuff and sniffed. "You might not be aware, Windermere, but the duchess does favor my suit. And it has not escaped my notice that His Grace is uncommonly swayed by his wife."

"Louisa?" Ned wanted to scoff. But glancing after her now, he saw her turn and give a friendly, departing wave to Levington.

"She's very grateful to me for saving her fair sister in the park the other day. Thought the whole episode sounded too romantic for words."

"Romantic? Hah!" Ned had to fight to hide his irritation. "You managed to take credit for that, did you?"

"The Lady Christina was all too willing to bestow it upon me, dear boy."

This was said in such a sly, snide manner, Ned felt a rush of temper, before he calmed himself with the words he himself had uttered concerning Robert.

"Drop it, Levington. You'll be wasting your time, and as I understand it, time is something you no longer have."

At this reminder of his near bankruptcy, Levington's smile turned nasty. "If I decide I want your advice, I'll be certain to ask for it."

Ned shrugged his anger off. Making his bow, he would have left the subject behind and gone in search of the cardroom right then, but Levington called him back.

"I don't suppose you've remembered the challenge that Grisham made you that same day?" he said.

Ned hid a wince. No, he had not remembered the challenge. Nor had he thought of sending his seconds, or even of appointing any friends to smooth the gentleman's ruffled feathers.

"He's been wondering if you are a coward," Levington continued, "however, as his second I have assured him of your eagerness to meet any gentleman in an affair of honor. May I tell him the names of your friends?"

Damn and blast! Ned had been sure his friend Carnes could talk Grisham out of a meeting, but after this second slight that would clearly be impossible. To offend a man was one thing. To fail to respond to his challenge was another matter entirely, one that could not be forgiven. Besides, if Ned failed to meet him now, Levington would spread it about that Ned had lost his nerve.

He must be getting old, if a simple thing like a spoiled girl's impudence could make him forget he'd been challenged to a duel. For he had completely forgotten as he'd lain in his bed last night, thinking about Robert's minx of a sister and how he'd trespassed on her innocence. He'd been afraid he'd awakened a touch of the passion he'd sensed in himself when he'd tasted her finger.

And, now, look where his concern had got him. Christina was off dancing a Scottish reel without a worry in her head, and he would have to be pacing off steps at dawn.

"You can call upon Lord Haynes and Rupert Carnes. I am sure they'll act for me. If I don't have time to speak with them myself, you can tell them I'm prepared to go with any weapon they suggest. I'd prefer not to make this a killing affair, however."

Levington bowed himself away with a smug grin, presumably to go in search of a partner, and Ned turned toward the cardroom with relief.

Christina had been mortified by Ned's obvious indifference after what had passed between them in the nursery. All evening his air had been that of the man she had met at the christening, the jaded rake, obliged by his friendship with Robert to accompany a tiresome ingenue to her first ton event.

She had promised Levington those dances, hoping to inspire a reaction from Ned, but instead, Robert had been the one to take umbrage. He had lectured her under his breath on the impropriety of encouraging any man introduced to her by Ned.

In spite of Christina's pique, she could not help feeling the injustice of Robert's words. Ned had not contrived the meeting between herself and Levington. He had presented the baron only when good manners had forced him to do so.

Her anger at this precise moment, however, did prevent her from defending Ned aloud, before she was presented to Robert's friend, Lord Buffington.

Pale in coloring, and possessed of a self-satisfied air and a thickening waist, Lord Buffington made her a dignified bow while brushing his lips across her fingers. Christina politely freed her hand from his moist, lingering grasp only to note Robert's beaming countenance as he observed the dry success of their meeting. Sensing at once that this was the man her brother had chosen for her, she did her best not to blanch.

"My mother, who was the Lady Mary Lawrence before she married my father, the first earl, has long been acquainted with your family," Buffington said. "She and your mother were bosom playmates as children, and she has always held that there is no one more versed in the polite tenets of Society than the Dowager Duchess of Broughton."

"Indeed." Christina found herself unable to think of a suitable rejoinder. Nor could she contradict his speech, since he had given an accurate description of her mother.

"Christina has just emerged from a ladies' seminary in

Bath, which my mother chose for her." Robert made this pronouncement as if it should be cause for applause.

"So I have heard." Buffington apparently thought it was, for he congratulated her on the accomplishments certain to have been derived from such excellent instruction. "Dare I hope to be permitted to witness one of said talents this evening? Perhaps in the next set?"

It took Christina a moment to realize that his arch query had been an invitation to dance. No doubt she had failed to acquire at her school a perfect understanding of the circuitous speeches that might be employed by a gentleman.

She saw that Robert was near to bursting a button on his waistcoat by the time she responded with a yes. She could do nothing else. Lord Buffington, for all his pomposity, meant to be an agreeable companion. It was not his fault that she found him such a bore.

Or perhaps it was, she later thought, as he proceeded to talk about himself and nothing else during a lively Scottish reel. Christina could only be glad that its frequent glides and circular patterns made conversation quite difficult.

It was during one of these rapid trips down the floor that she spied Ned leaving the assembly room without a passing glance at either her or her partner.

Christina felt the betrayal much more than she wanted to admit. How dare he leave the room without so much as a country dance with either her or Louisa? And why should he be able to quit the dance when he wished, when she was bound and gagged by it?

Ned was a rake; that was why. Rakes could do anything they pleased, and everyone else had to accept their choices. But let a young lady flaunt the tiniest element of a convention and she was deemed beyond salvation.

The anger these thoughts aroused must have flashed in

her eyes, for after one glance at her face, Lord Buffington stumbled. Quickly, Christina pasted on her brightest smile, and the young gentleman recovered.

On their next turn, she spied Lord Levington awaiting their dance together. He inclined his head as she passed, the naked gleam in his eye leaving her in no doubt that it was she he had come to dance with this evening.

Christina fought the immediate temptation to give him a set-down, and instead bestowed a sultry smile.

If Ned had no wish to dance with her, she would make another use of her time.

Chapter Five

*N*ed stayed in the cardroom, submerged in the game while trying his best to ignore the strains of music issuing from the adjoining salon. It was not until Robert appeared at his side, considerably vexed and asking to speak with him in private, that he allowed himself the luxury of looking up.

He excused himself from the table, and they stepped a few paces away into a quiet corner.

"What's wrong?" Ned asked. "You look as if you're about to be stricken by a fit of apoplexy. I suggest a few deep breaths."

"It's Levington." Robert's face was as grim as his tone. "He just finished dancing two dances with Christina, and, if this evening's work ruins her, I shall have you to thank."

Ned ignored the worry invading his chest. "You must be exaggerating," he said. "What could Levington possibly do to ruin Christina on the floor of Almack's?"

"It's what he'd *like* to do that is all too obvious." Robert raked trembling fingers through his thinning hair. "He makes no attempt to hide his strong attraction. I almost think he's trying to scare off any other suitors before they even have a chance to meet her. It's indecent how the fellow looks her over. And"—Robert's voice held a note of desperation—"as impossible as it sounds, especially when she could nab a superior fellow like

Buffington with just a little push, Christina seems to be responding to Levington's overtures."

"He's seducing her on the dance floor?" Ned raised a brow. "He has more talent than I gave him credit for."

"It's all very well from where you are sitting," Robert snapped. "Go ahead and laugh. But she is my sister, Ned, and people have already remarked her partiality for the scoundrel. I tell you, this will ruin her chances with Buffington if he hears the whispers that are circulating."

"Then Buffington is a fool who deserves to lose his chance with *her*." Ned shrugged with a nonchalance he did not feel. He was the one who had introduced Christina to Levington, albeit unintentionally, and he knew Levington could be dangerous. He supposed he would have to do something to discourage her from making a grave mistake.

Maintaining an air of extreme detachment, he allowed Robert to lead him back to the assembly room in time to see the couples forming the next set.

It took him only a moment to locate Christina. Levington had her by the arm and was about to walk her out onto the floor.

Ned gave a start. He asked quickly, "How many times did you say those two have danced?"

"Twice," Robert said, before he spied them making their way into position. "Oh, my God!"

"Precisely." This last was said through clenched teeth, as, leaving Robert behind, Ned made his way through the assembly. He intercepted the two miscreants in the middle of the floor before the music had a chance to start.

Christina glanced his way and a guilty flush, mixed with a spark of some brighter emotion, touched her face.

"Kind of you to escort my partner onto the floor, Levington," Ned said smoothly, following his statement with a bow and an arm quickly offered to Christina. "Shocking, is it not, how difficult these crushes make it for one to find one's next partner?"

Before Levington could utter his protest, Ned took a step his way and, in a silky voice, said, "His Grace of Broughton expressly requested me to prevent this spectacle from occurring. If you care to discuss his feelings on the subject of your conduct with his sister, I suggest you take it up with him right now."

Levington halted with his mouth half open to speak. With a hasty glance, he found Robert hovering on the side of the floor. Ned did not have to turn around to see the formidable expression on Robert's face.

With barely a second's hesitation, Levington put on his most gracious smile and, making his leg to Christina, left her in Ned's capable hands.

Christina appeared to suppress a flinch, as Ned turned to direct her a reproachful look.

"My dear little fool," he said, smiling pleasantly for the crowd. "Are you truly unaware of the error you were about to make?"

"Error, my lord?" Christina's toothy smile was as patently false as his.

"Correction. Errors." Only then, as the music had started, had he recognized the opening notes of a waltz. "May I presume that in addition to granting that gentleman a third dance, you also neglected to obtain the hostesses' permission to waltz?"

"You may. But what if I told you I do not recognize the hostesses' authority over my choice either of dance or of partner?" Christina could not say this without a note of frustration.

Ned's lips curved, and his eyes held more than a touch of sympathy as he again offered her his arm, but he refused to allow her the same code of conduct he allowed himself.

"Minx," was all he said as he calmly ushered her off the floor.

When Ned did not head for one of the patronesses to ask permission to waltz with her but, instead, led her to a refreshment table, she balked. "Where are we going?"

"To obtain a glass of orgeat. I think you stand in need of a dose."

"I did not come here to be doctored with barley water, thank you. I came to enjoy the dance, which to most people means to waltz."

"With Levington? You could do a sight better than him."

"If you are so certain, I am surprised you do not dance with me yourself."

"And entertain the gossips? No, my dear. And do not flatter yourself. I was not offering my services as partner."

"If you meant Lord Buffington, then I warn you I just might scream."

Ned made a choking sound before patting her hand. His own was warm and, as his palm brushed the tops of her fingers, Christina felt suddenly alive.

"Never fear." His voice was intimate, and it held a surprising degree of comfort. "I'm certain Lord Buffington has already been frightened off. According to your prostrated brother, my dear friend Robert, Lord Levington has ogled you so thoroughly in front of this gathering as even to raise a blush under Buffington's dense skin."

Christina fought a prickling of shame, as he added, "A model of propriety like Buffington would never stand to see a lady he meant to wed flirting with any other gentleman. It would be a wound to his highly inflated opinion of himself. I take it you were flirting?"

Christina ignored Ned's teasing question to pose one of her own. "And you would?"

"Would what?"

"Would let the lady you intended to marry flirt shamelessly with another man?"

"We are not discussing me."

"Oh? Why must we discuss all my failings and never yours?"

Ned gave her a look that contained more than a hint of bitterness. "Because," he said, halting in his stride to look darkly down at her, "I have been the object of so much scandal these past many years that my sins are now a matter of public record. Yours are not, most thankfully, yet. But if you continue in this headstrong manner, they soon will be, and I doubt it shall make you happy."

With an averted glance, he quickly changed the subject. "Where is Louisa? Shouldn't she be taking better care of you than this?"

"I doubt she feels needed, since you and Robert are doing such a splendid job."

When Ned did not reply, but kept searching the room for her sister-in-law, Christina added, "I'm not sure where she's gone." His reluctance either to sit and bear her company or to dance with her wounded her pride and made her determined to annoy him again. "I'm afraid she might have come down with a headache. Why don't you inquire outside the ladies' withdrawing room, while I wait for you here?"

Ned showed a glimmer of appreciation for her attempted ruse. "Sorry. Afraid I won't fall for that one."

"Then, if you do not mean to dance, I wish you would introduce me to one of your friends."

"My friends do not haunt Almack's."

"All the better. I have found this company to be uninspired, despite its exalted reputation."

His glimmer changed to a frown, which he attempted to hide before raking the assembly room again with his gaze. "Where could Louisa be? I shall have to take you to Robert, which you shan't like. But I cannot have you standing near me all the time, not after you've already got people talking about you and Levington."

"Are you afraid they will gossip about you and me?"

Ned glanced at her sharply. "I do not think you have been listening. I know you've been buried in the wilds of Bath, but let me inform you, Lady Chris, I am not someone you should be seen with very often. If at all."

Christina bestowed an indulgent smile upon him. "Coming it a bit too brown, aren't you, Ned? What harm could you possibly do me at Almack's?"

At that very moment the music halted, throwing them into a relative quiet.

Ned turned, and in his eyes she saw a hint of the electricity that had passed between them the day before.

He let his gaze comb her slowly from her toes to her head. Christina felt a heat spreading slowly under her clothes.

He moved a step closer, until their right sides nearly touched, and the breath from his lips teased the hair near her ear. "I could do you every bit as much harm as Levington could." His voice rose barely above a whisper. "Do not doubt it for a moment."

As her lips fell open, he turned abruptly to lead her back to Robert. A pulse had quickened in her throat. All at once, Almack's had become so much more interesting.

But she couldn't leave matters the way they were, or Ned would continue to avoid her—as he clearly meant to do.

"Lord Levington has promised to show me some of the sights of London," she said, tripping along behind Ned.

"Robert will never allow it."

She grinned and replied with a confident little air, "Oh, Robert's wishes never concern me overmuch. I suspect we shall contrive a way."

As Ned was spinning to face her, Louisa appeared in a flurry of green and gold satin, nearly out of breath.

"Oh, there you are, my dears. I am so happy to have found you at last. Robert and I have been separated this hour and more. But, you see, someone stepped on the hem of my skirt, and the maid in the ladies' withdrawing room began to tell me all about her sister, poor girl, who has got herself in the most distressing predicament, and I was telling her about one of my charities I thought might help.

"I am so sorry, Christina," she apologized. "I hope you have been sufficiently entertained and have had some interesting partners?"

"Yes, I have," was all Christina said, as she gloated over Ned's discomfiture. Before Louisa had spoken, Christina had caught a glimpse of his furious glare. It had burned a hole right through her. She knew he was madly itching to discover just what she'd meant when she'd said she and Lord Levington would contrive.

He did nothing about it, however. With Louisa's appearance, his manner had reverted at once to that of the long-suffering escort, and he scarcely glanced at Christina again except to bid her a cool good-night.

Of course, Christina told herself later in bed, he could not continue treating her like a naughty schoolgirl caught sneaking out of the drawing-master's room, not in front of Louisa and Robert, at least. Neither had the faintest notion of the terms she was on with Ned.

Not that she was altogether certain she knew what those terms were herself. His attempts on the one hand to regulate her deportment revealed something more than the world-weary rake, while his determined steps to frighten her off had had quite the opposite effect.

Perhaps he thought that heated looks and a low, threatening voice, carefully designed to incite lustful feelings, would intimidate an innocent like her with the hint of dangers she knew nothing of. Well, Ned would discover that she was made of sterner stuff.

Christina wondered what she could do to annoy him next. She had certainly managed to stir him out of his insufferable arrogance. The worst thing she could do just now would be to rest. Without Ned to tease, the evening at Almack's would have passed with intolerable tedium, and Christina was not ready to resign herself to a life filled with that.

Well, she thought to herself, slipping down into the sheets with a sense of some accomplishment, she would simply have to see. If Ned could not be provoked by her actions at the next gathering they attended, she could always attach herself firmly to Robert Edward, and Ned would be frustrated into rage.

The thought of his rage, and the form it might take, lured her into a delicious sleep.

The next many days saw an increase in the number of their social engagements. Christina was duly presented at Court and made her curtsy.

Fortunately, for Robert's sake, she managed to evade the Regent's eye, for His Highness always preferred a woman of ampler girth. Not that Robert had feared the Regent would make seriously improper advances to the sister of one as highly born as he, but he would not have relished the gossip if Christina had taken it into her head to flirt with the Prince.

For now that she was on the Town, Robert's worries followed him every night and on into every morning, so that he could hardly get a decent night's sleep. If he and Louisa did not watch the girl carefully, she was certain to do something to cause them to blanch. At least, Robert reflected with justifiable incense, *he* always blanched. Louisa apparently experienced no such anxiety over Christina's reputation. She'd already informed him it would be his task to find Christina the appropriate partner since he had already refused to consider Louisa's two candidates.

No reasonable (or, for that matter, unreasonable) amount of discussion had convinced Louisa that her first two choices—Ned and Levington, for God's sake—were entirely out of the question.

Robert began to regret that Louisa had ever made the offer to bring Christina out. He missed their quiet evenings spent together at home. This running after Christina and watching whom she danced with and how many times, whom she met, and whom she sat down to dinner with was wearing him out. Fortunately, now that Robert knew that Ned had no interest in his sister, he could trust him to take on some of the burden.

It had been wonderful really, Robert reflected to himself one night before his dinner guests arrived, how Ned had become such a reliable friend, ever since Robert had confided to him his lack of confidence in Louisa as a chaperon. Ned had forsaken some of his own pursuits to stand by Robert in his time of need.

The first time Robert had spotted Ned at a ball on an evening he would normally have spent at the opera or at cards, he had been grateful for Ned's willingness to share the task of mounting guard over Christina. Not that Robert had ever asked Ned to play at duenna. But the second Christina's partner had crossed the line between polite flirtation and insolence, Ned had been quick to step in. He'd prevented them from seeking a private interview behind a pair of heavy curtains, before Robert had even realized the couple's intent. Robert could only assume that Ned's superior experience in clandestine affairs—he had so often been the perpetrator of scandals himself—had led him to form an instinct that allowed him to predict such occurrences before they actually transpired.

How else to explain Ned's quickness anytime Christina stood in danger of exposing herself to public censure?

Robert found that his question begged an answer of its own.

Why *was* Ned spending so many of his evenings in their company? He never had been one to attend affairs at which the principle guests would be the Season's giggling debutantes—not since his disastrous first year on the Town, when he'd crossed the line too many times to count. Nor had he expressed an interest in any member of this year's crop of ingenues. At least, as Robert recalled, Ned had not done much dancing, not above two or three sets in an evening, and always with different girls.

Instead, Ned had spent most of his time at these affairs strolling about the rooms, stopping to speak to a friend every now and then, while his watchful gaze swept the crowd. If he indulged in a hand of cards, he was always certain to be back, scanning the ballroom again within half an hour.

The more Robert thought about Ned's recent change in behavior, the more he thought it was deucedly odd.

"I say, Louisa," he said, as she stepped into her evening gown. He had been sitting in the armchair in her boudoir, taking a few minutes of pleasure in watching her dress. "Are you absolutely certain that Ned has no interest in Christina at all?"

After a surprised tilt of her head, Louisa gave him an indulgent laugh. "Of course, I cannot be certain unless I ask him directly. And from what I understood, that subject was to be closed. Why do you ask? Have you noticed any signs that he is?"

Robert had no wish to encourage Louisa in this direction, so he temporized. "No, no. I was merely curious as to why he seems to have given up his usual entertainments so very often to attend the same functions as we."

"Ahhhh, yes," Louisa said, nodding with understanding now. "I suppose that should make you wonder. But, do you know, Robert dear, I think our friend Ned has grown rather weary of his style of life. Why else would he take such an interest in Robert Edward? And if he has formed an equal concern for Christina's welfare—not that there is any need, of course—why, we should do nothing to discourage him. You know how many hazards Society can pose to a young lady. Perhaps Ned is merely exercising the paternal feelings he has no other way to indulge."

Robert was not so certain. He couldn't imagine any gentleman showing this much concern for his friend's younger sister. Especially Ned.

He stood and paced. But all he said was, "I suppose you could be right."

Louisa seemed to detect his uneasiness. "If you seriously doubt his intentions, I could always change my seating arrangements for this evening. I had intended to put Christina next to Ned. It is a logical placement with respect to rank, but I had chiefly designed that seating to avoid putting her next to Lord Wimbly. His hands are inclined to wander."

"Wander?" Robert's eyebrows shot up. "Wander where?"

"Oh . . ." Louisa's manner was evasive. "Wherever he wants them to, I suppose."

"You've never told me this about Wimbly. And I am positive you have been seated next to him a dozen times or more at dinner."

His accusing stare made her pause. "My dear, if I informed you of the indelicate behavior of every gentleman I met, you would likely spend the rest of your life defending my honor. I should never again enjoy your company at dawn."

Robert felt the blood draining from his face. "I never realized," he said. And here he had been running after Christina, when his beloved wife had been repeatedly subject to insult. He would have to keep a closer eye on Louisa from now on.

"No, don't move Ned," he said, resigning himself to the inevitable need of Ned's assistance. "I daresay he can be trusted."

"Certainly he can." Louisa joined him near the door. "I have no doubt of Ned's good intentions. You may leave those to me."

That evening, when Ned arrived at Broughton House and handed over his hat and coat to the footman, he felt nearly as wrung out as Robert at the prospect of another evening watching Christina. He waited in the foyer with the other guests preparing to enter the drawing room and took a deep, fortifying breath. At least this event was to be nothing more trying than a formal dinner.

Thank heavens it was not a ball. At a large gathering, the little minx could think of a dozen ways to risk embarrassing herself. If Ned had not kept his eyes firmly open, she would have done so many more times than he wished to count.

Robert had no notion of the number of occasions Ned had been obliged to prevent an incident that would have ruined his sister. Concerned as Robert was by her "ill-considered judgment," he seemed to have no idea that the girl was not what she appeared. Beneath that crown of angel's hair and behind those clear blue eyes churned the unrepentant mind of a hoyden. Christina seemed determined to flaunt Society's norms, as if she wished to dispense with the whole rigid mess.

In spite of the dozens of eligible bachelors Robert had tried to put in her way, Christina persisted in being most attracted to the wastrels who made a practice of hanging out for heiresses, those men who made it a profession to be oily. She had an uncanny talent for attracting them to her side. While most of these men would have taken a shot at their prospects with her anyway, they had received nothing but encouragement from Christina herself. Ned couldn't decide whether she truly believed their lies or if she took a perverse satisfaction from putting herself at risk. Whatever the case, she actually seemed pleased when one of her dancing partners turned out to be a rake.

Ned had been forced to use all his diplomatic skills to avoid another meeting like the one with Grisham in which Ned had nearly lost a leg. They had faced each other on the heath in the hour of a cold, dreary dawn. Ned's head had been aching from Christina's antics the night before, and he had barely paid his adversary any mind.

Fortunately, in trying to cripple rather than kill him, Grisham had chosen a narrow target—Ned's knee. The bullet had barely grazed Ned's thigh. Ned, who knew he had been in the wrong, had aimed for the other man's right arm in the hope of spoiling his shot. Adept at the duello, Ned had often used this technique.

His unexpected miss had driven home the possibility that he might have died on the field. Grisham and he had both ridden away from the incident, but Ned had no particular wish to repeat the events of that morning.

If he had been killed, he'd wondered later, who would have made sure that Christina did not do something foolish to ruin herself that night?

Angry with her for getting him into such a dangerous situation, he had even tried to think of a worthy husband for her. Ned had found, however, that he knew few worthy men. If a candidate did suggest himself, Ned soon found an irrefutable reason for rejecting him. Either the prospect would have some failing no sister of Robert's should have to accept or else Ned would decide the man was simply too weak to govern her as he should.

And throughout all these travails, Ned had refrained from telling Robert just how serious the girl's antics had become. He knew that Robert's reaction would be extreme, possibly cruel. He would undoubtedly pack Christina off to live with the dowager again, which was a fate Ned would not wish on anyone.

He might have confided his private concerns to Louisa, but she seemed to dote on Christina so much, Ned did not want to be the one to inform her what a graceless scamp the girl was. He knew too well how painful rejection by a near relation could be.

In that moment, he entered the drawing room, where the family was greeting their guests, and put his thoughts aside.

"Dear, dear Ned."

As she spied him and held out her hands, Louisa's warm, welcoming voice acted like a balm.

Ned had always envied Robert that warmth. Sometimes, when he allowed himself to think of such things, he wondered what it would be like to have the force of a woman's love directed solely at him. Then he always reminded himself that since he was not in love with any woman, he would surely tire of the cloying attention.

He had never kept a mistress for that reason, preferring to amuse himself with less onerous flings. But, tonight, he found himself wondering about a constant love again.

"Louisa."

Ned kissed her hand and held on to it a second longer than was proper merely to annoy Robert, who was standing by her side. Then he glanced at Christina, who had been greeting another guest as Ned had entered and only now looked up.

Expecting to be met with her usual challenging gaze,

he had meant to find some way to tease her. He'd been searching for a probing phrase to rouse her ire. But he was taken aback and then dismayed to see that dark circles had formed under her eyes. Christina's fair coloring gave away most of her feelings. At the moment, her face had the pale cast of sheepskin, with its delicate veins and brittle texture exposed to the light. This dangerous game she had been playing seemed to have done her more harm than he'd thought.

Her cheeks had none of their usual bloom, no matter how perfectly the light blue of her dress enhanced her eyes, and the soft white glow of her pearls matched the color of her breast. Her cheer seemed listless and forced.

She rallied, though, as soon as she saw him. Her back became straighter, and she lifted her chin before acknowledging his bow with a tantalizing smile. Alert to her tricks, Ned wondered what thought could be behind her angled glance and curving lips. Some deviltry, he was certain. But what would it be tonight?

Louisa's dinner party consisted of several men in the government with Robert, along with Louisa's particular set of friends. Normally, Ned would not have made one of this company, but he assumed his status as Robert Edward's godfather had given him a permanent legitimacy in this house. As he thought of Little Ned now, he wished he could retire to the nursery to watch the baby struggle to roll himself heels over head.

The episode with Christina in the nursery had changed the aspect of that haven, however. Ned could not step into it again without wondering if she might appear.

She had not given away his secret. For that he was grateful.

The company soon gathered for dinner around a long mahogany table, lit by a pair of magnificent chandeliers and laid with gilt-rimmed porcelain. As the footman guided Ned to his place near the center of one long side, he was astonished to find Christina already seated to the right of his chair.

Startled by this arrangement, he was unprepared to school his features. His reaction astonished him, as his pulse gave a leap and a smile welled up from deep inside.

Christina's expression, which had been composed, underwent a subtle change, as if a shy, little flame had flickered inside her.

Ned quickly recovered his composure and accepted the footman's help with his chair. His pulse, however, still raced.

It must be due to the game they'd been playing, he decided. There was a certain thrill, a sort of heightened chase, in his intercourse with Christina. Nothing so risky as an affair, of course, but there had been an element of intrigue in the way they had managed to hide their particular brand of intimacy from everyone else. In front of Robert, and now surrounded by his guests, they would have to play the part of polite acquaintances—when in truth, little between them had been polite.

What the assembled company would think if they knew the sort of conversations he had enjoyed with Christina, Ned could only imagine. They would be scandalized, that was certain. He could merely assume it was this latent shock, threatening to wake at the slightest slip of a tongue, that gave such spice to all their dealings.

Ned ignored the niggling feeling that something in this diagnosis was not right, as he lowered his voice to speak. "My dear Lady Christina, how delightful to have your company at dinner."

"Thank you, my lord. Does the arrangement astonish you as much as it does me?"

"Not at all," Ned said.

Although it did. Now that he thought of it, he could not

imagine what had got into Robert. A rise in the voices of the other guests allowed him to add for her benefit alone, "Your brother has come to regard me as your guardian angel, I believe. But even Robert has no idea of the truth. I daresay if he did, he would pack you back to Bath at once."

"You will not tell him, however."

"If I were you, I should not be so certain. Come to think of it, you would probably benefit from more schooling. Tell me, did you listen to anything your masters told you?"

"Certainly. My instructor on the pianoforte thought I had the best ear for music he had ever encountered."

"Oh?"

"Yes. He played me love songs. Unfortunately, this gave me little time on the instrument myself."

Ned stifled a choke before Christina's attention was begged by Lord Albemarle on her right. Ned found himself forced to entertain the Duchess of Gant on his left.

The Duchess longed to discuss Ned's ancestry, which somewhere in the seventeenth century contained a relative of her own. Ned was saved from this lengthy chronicling only during those times that Louisa decided to entertain the gentleman on her left. Unfortunately, her most loquacious guest was to her right, which kept the other ladies' heads turned in that direction.

Ned's dinner conversation proceeded in this unequal fashion: long tastes of a drab sort of course followed by short, spicy tidbits of dessert.

Lord Albemarle was young, but a gloomy kind of peer. A poet with a philanthropist's heart, he and Louisa had been involved in several of the same causes—a virtue Christina tried to appreciate as she listened to him agonizing over the dismal conditions to be found in burgeoning cities like Leeds and Manchester.

Knowing nothing of those towns herself and incapable of doing anything to relieve them, Christina quickly found her tolerance for pity being sadly overwhelmed. The relief she found, when occasionally she was able to turn toward Ned, made it hard to conceal her delight at the sight of his laughing eyes.

Under the cover of clinking spoons and clattering china, Ned expressed his regret that Her Grace of Gant could not have been seated next to Lord Buffington, "for they would have found much to go on together about."

His voice was so low, Christina was obliged to lean his way to hear. As their shoulders touched, for the space of a tiny moment, she felt as if there were no one in the room but themselves.

"He is quite devoted to family trees, is he not?" Ned continued, forgetting to eat his trifle as he scanned the room. "But I do not see Buffington. Was he not invited?"

"Oh, yes, he was," Christina replied with a conspiratorial grin, "but I am afraid Lord Buffington has lost interest in blending our two distinguished families, and since he's as rich as Croesus, he can afford to turn up his nose at my attractive dowry. From what Robert tells me, he was rather alarmed to detect a sign of high spirits in me. He fears that too much spirit in a female is evidence of a bad strain in the line."

"The fool."

Ned's simple response, uttered halfway between anger and contempt, provoked a surge in Christina's heart. The feeling was so acute and unexpected, she was at pains to hide the tears that sprang into her eyes.

When Robert had reported Buffington's remark, he had clearly taken the gentleman's side and had expressed his hope that Christina would learn from this rejection what she must do to improve her deportment if she wanted to catch a prize such as Buffington.

Ned's unequivocal opinion seemed a confirmation of her rights, even a tacit approval of who she was. No one but Louisa had ever offered her such a gift, and Louisa did not really know her.

But Ned did. Or, at least, he was privy to the worst of her actions. As a rake, she supposed, he could not truly be shocked by anything she'd done. The only trouble was she had not been happy with her actions of late. Not that she had often been delighted with herself, outside the occasional burst of triumph at besting an adversary, and the few precious times she had put Robert Edward to sleep.

But, for the most part, since coming to London she had felt out of control, as if she were riding downhill on a runaway sleigh, grasping hard to the seat to stay on, but certain of plunging off a cliff.

"Don't let that pompous windbag cast you down." Ned's gaze moved swiftly to her face and then away. They were speaking softly so that no one at the table could overhear.

Starting, Christina realized he must have noticed her tears. For the moment, his hard, teasing look was gone, and she caught a glimpse of the boy who had comforted her so long ago.

Then he spoiled the moment by saying, with an irritable jerk of his head, "There are far worthier gentlemen who will relish your high spirits. I am sure you will find happiness with one of them."

"Thank you, my lord." Christina did her best to hide her sharp disappointment. So, Ned, like Robert, thought she ought to find a *worthy* gentleman to marry, did he? Well, she would soon disabuse him of that notion.

"You are too kind, my lord. However, I find that *un*worthy gentlemen are usually more to my taste."

Ned's brows snapped together in a frown. "You are not still encouraging that fortune hunter Levington, are you?"

"Why not? I have a fortune of my own."

"Which shall be eaten up before you see twenty-five if Levington ever gets his hands upon it."

"Really? But how can one be sure? Do you not think we should give Lord Levington the benefit of the doubt? He seems quite devoted to me, so perhaps he would turn over a new leaf. And as humdrum as that seems, it would probably be the best thing for the children."

"Children? What children?" Ned seemed to blanch.

"My lord, you will surely make me blush if you ask me to explain the inevitable consequences of marriage."

"Christina, I'm warning you. . . ."

"Now," she said delightedly, "you are sounding just like Robert, when I had thought you a rogue. Amazing how age can turn even the most dangerous men into models of propriety. I wonder if Levington will turn respectable when he is one-and-thirty?"

"He is *six*-and-thirty now." Ned spoke between clenched teeth. "And getting desperate, I see, if he is bothering to lie about his age."

Christina held the sudden urge to giggle at the sight of Ned's tightly controlled fury. "Is he truly?" was all she said. "Well, I have always loved an older man."

"Always?" Ned's tone expressed his incredulity. "Coming it much too brown, my dear. You've never been in love, or my name is Buffington. Nor can you convince me that Levington has won your heart."

"Ahhhh . . ." Christina formulated her response on a long, drawn-out breath. "Perhaps you are right, and I am only temporarily dazzled. But then, Levington is always so willing to give me what I want."

"And what is that?"

A footman stepped between them to serve the final course, and Ned's frustration could be read in the tense line of his mouth.

As soon as the footman disappeared, Christina leaned closer to Ned, with a surreptitious glance back at Robert.

Fortunately, he did not seem to be paying her and Ned the slightest mind.

"What I want is to be taken to one of those gaming houses you undoubtedly frequent in Pall Mall."

If she had expected to be rewarded with a flash of anger or even amusement, she was quickly disappointed. Ned's eyes were as sober as the set of his jaw, when he replied, "You would never do anything so stupid."

"Why not? I am sure you do stupid things all the time."

She saw that she had taken him aback with her logic. "You might even offer to take me to one yourself, if you think Lord Levington is not to be trusted. As good a friend as you've become, I am sure *you* can be trusted."

"Don't be absurd. You are acting like a brat."

Christina felt all the truth of his words, but still she could not help herself. Ignoring a pressing ache inside, she shrugged as charmingly as she could. "Very well," she promised lightly. "If you will not take me, I shall simply ask Levington."

A gleam of intelligence relieved Ned's stormy visage. His unyielding posture relaxed. "This is all bluff," he said, speaking through a grin. "You will never be able to leave the house without someone's being aware."

"Dear, dear Ned." With a little chuckle, Christina shook her head at his innocence. "Has no one ever told you of windows? I assure you I know how to make full use of mine."

Just then, Christina's gloomy neighbor tapped her on the shoulder in order to finish his monologue on factory conditions, which had been interrupted on their last switch of partners. With a dazzling smile she did not feel, Christina turned her back on Ned.

Chapter Six

*N*ed left the dinner party that evening, worried that he had underestimated Christina's desire to do herself in. Her threat, that she would make Levington take her to a place she had no business going, had sounded an alarm. While she had threatened many pranks before, none had approached this degree of seriousness.

All along, Ned had wondered what sort of demon was driving her to practice such impropriety. He'd doubted that she could receive much gratification from her acts. And yet, she persisted in thinking up ways to court social ruin.

At first, he reluctantly confessed to himself, he'd found her brand of girlish impudence entertaining. He had not truly minded keeping an eye out for her interest, not when her clever powers of invention had posed such a challenge. It had almost seemed as if they'd joined in a battle of wits. He had let Christina know he would not allow her antics to pass the bounds, and Christina in turn had done her damnedest to confound his efforts to guard her reputation. Their constant dueling over Society's rules, a thing they commonly despised, had actually brought them into friendship, he'd thought.

Ned could not deny their fellow feeling, nor his sympathy for a girl with such high spirits being forced to play the simpering miss. Nor did he seriously deny his growing interest in her welfare.

But this last start, the one she had so casually mentioned tonight, was of an entirely different sort from the others. Ned wondered if he could dismiss it as merely an idle threat. She might have uttered it in an attempt to tease him. He had not failed to notice the pleasure she took in raising his temper.

But the trouble was her threat had not seemed idle. How she could even contemplate such an action—not only outrageous by anyone's standards, but of serious danger to herself—had disturbed him all evening.

A voice in the back of his head tried to tell him he had often behaved the same, but Ned rejected this notion outright. Christina was a very young female, with kind relations, a proper education, and a woman's sensibilities. She could not possibly be suffering from the same dark restlessness he had known all his life.

Nevertheless, she'd appeared to be suffering from something tonight. Her wan coloring and the glint of desperation he'd detected in her eyes had sent him a signal he could ill afford to ignore.

He knew he ought to tell Robert. But would Robert believe his sister was threatening to go to a gambling hell, or would he reasonably suspect Ned to be out of his mind? The notion that a delicately raised female would contemplate such lunacy was not one a man usually threw at the girl's brother. Not unless he wanted to meet that brother at dawn.

Ned sighed heavily over the prospect of offending Robert to that degree. No, he would do better to watch out for the chit himself to make sure the proposition she'd made remained so much idle bluff.

* * *

Over the next many nights, he stayed alert to Christina's whereabouts. In the course of normal events, this was actually quite easy. They were certain to be invited to the same affairs. At the height of the Season, the list of balls and parties was entirely predictable to one with Ned's social expertise.

If a ball was in the offing, he could check to make certain Christina had arrived and that she was being properly chaperoned. If the evening called for the theater, he had only to sit where he could spy Robert's box to reassure himself that nothing was afoot.

In the meantime, however, as a result of this private concern, which was causing him an unanticipated amount of anguish, he decided to avoid Christina as much as he could. Her most outrageous acts often seemed provoked by his presence, as if the pleasure she took in thwarting him were part of her reason for misbehaving. It was all part of their game, he thought. But if, in playing, she had lost control, Ned would have no part of feeding her waywardness.

Christina's high spirits, though they stirred his blood with their youth and daring, could have no permanent place in her future. She must marry. Even though she revolted at the very notion of pleasing an eligible man, she must soon reconcile herself to that necessity.

She would not wish to remain childless and a spinster. It was time she woke up to the risk of losing all chance of matrimonial harmony.

Ned could only wonder what was wrong with all the young bucks these days that no one suitable had seen what a prize she would make and fought for the pleasure of making her his.

He continued his vigilance, forsaking his clubs and his gambling hells in the possibility that Christina would try to visit one herself. Ned paid particular attention whenever Levington was about. Even though the baron's visits had been politely discouraged from Broughton House, Robert had found no legitimate way to keep Christina from speaking to him at functions they attended.

Forewarned by his mistake at Almack's that night, Levington had altered his tactics and become the very model of propriety in order to win Robert's heart. As a result of Levington's moderation, Robert had begun to worry less about him than about some of Christina's other suitors and had consequently lowered his guard.

During the week following Louisa's dinner, Ned spotted Levington several times in Christina's company. More than once, they seemed disturbingly intent upon a private conversation, and Ned could not find a way to come between them without giving the appearance of someone more concerned than he wished to seem. But nothing scandalous had yet occurred.

Then, just as he'd begun to feel that his extreme care in guarding the girl had been unjustified, Christina failed to appear at a ball to which she had been invited.

Robert and Louisa had come. As soon as Ned spied them entering the vast drawing room, he casually scanned the corridor behind them for Christina as well. But no amount of searching uncovered her whereabouts, so he was forced to ask Robert where she was.

"Christina came down with a headache just before we departed this evening and declared she could not go," Robert said with a sigh. "Frankly, I think she has had enough of parties for the instant. I dashed well know I have myself."

"Then why did you not stay at home to bear her company?" Ned tried to muffle his concern, but the sight of Robert without his wayward sister had alarmed him.

Robert said wistfully, "I would have been more than happy to, but Louisa insisted we could not all disappoint

Lady Ensley. I would give anything to spend one quiet night at home, but no doubt she's right. I hope to get her out of here before too late, though."

"Will you look in on Christina when you get home?"

"No." Robert shook his head. "We promised not to disturb her. What she wants, she said, is a good night's rest. You know what the devil it can be to try to get back to sleep once one has been awakened."

"Of course."

Ned saw immediately that his uncertain tone had captured Robert's attention.

"What?" he said, a glimmer of worry taking birth in his eyes. "Why are you asking so many questions about Christina?"

"My dear Robert." Ned used the arrogance he knew so well how to employ. "You have asked me to keep an eye on the girl until I barely have an evening to myself. Now when I pose an innocent question about her health, you take me to task?"

His cool delivery calmed Robert, who said defensively, "Don't be so testy, Ned. Of course I'm not taking you to task. It was merely that for a moment—"

With a hasty frown, Robert refrained from pursuing the subject. Instead, he invited Ned to join him in the cardroom.

It took all the diplomacy Ned possessed to avoid being swept into a game, which would have tied him down for half an hour at least, without raising Robert's suspicions over his reluctance to play. It was entirely unlike him to turn down an invitation to cards, especially at a ball, which could offer him no other enjoyment.

But he was determined to discover whether Christina's headache was real.

A quick turn of the room, and then two more, decided him that Levington had not come to the ball. The baron's failure to appear at such an elegant event, certain to be attended by many heiresses ripe for plucking, did not bode well for Christina's story. Ned tried to reassure himself with the possible reasons for Levington's absence, but his unerring instinct pointed him toward only one.

He left Lady Ensley's party and hired a chair to carry him to Pall Mall, cursing himself for a misguided fool all the way.

Over the course of the next two hours, Ned searched the private gambling hells where Levington might have dared to take Christina. He wasted no time in discovering their directions because he had frequented them all himself. On a hunch, he ruled out the ones at which ladies of the evening were known to be in prevalence and opted instead for those at which hardened gamesters of both sexes might be found. He did not think that even Levington would be so foolish as to choose a place where Christina's virtue might be compromised.

The thought that the baron might well use the opportunity Christina had so innocently provided him to turn elopement into rape, with a consequent marriage, made Ned so feverish with anxiety that he found it hard to maintain a polite demeanor with the acquaintances he passed. Only by holding on to his cynicism, which told him Levington still cherished hopes of persuading Robert to sanction the marriage, could Ned conduct his search with any appearance of calm.

The first two houses, both on nearby side streets, offered no sign of the pair. But at the third, a private residence with an aging boxer standing guard at the door, Ned got lucky.

The owner of this hell, a former opera dancer with a trumped-up widowhood attached to her name, had invited her guests to partake of a masked supper tonight. The purpose of such disguises could only be to encourage the attendance of ladies who would normally fear to be seen in such an establishment. Masks would allow them to indulge their indiscretions without the consequences that would otherwise arise.

And to this particular assembly, Ned gratefully remarked as he made his way past the various tables in the dimly lit room, hazard and faro seemed to hold more allure than the opposite sex. Considering the anonymity of the group, surprisingly little in the way of flirting was going on. Instead, the guests remained intent upon their tables with all the passion of true gamesters.

One table in particular captured Ned's attention. This was due to the couple standing by it who appeared to be engaged in an escalating quarrel. The gentleman, whose artful brown locks looked plastered in place, was eager to resume his play, while his companion—a young lady with smooth, blond hair piled high upon her head—seemed out of spirits. Her colorless lips beneath a rose pink mask gave the lie to the stubborn set of her jaw.

Ned had no sooner recognized Christina than a rush of immense relief flowed through his body—followed quickly by a deadly rage. Despite an inner voice that urged him to relish her discomfort a moment more, he couldn't contain his temper any longer. A few hasty strides brought him to within inches of the pair.

As they turned, startled by his sudden assault, he began, "You will pardon me, my lady, but I must inform you that it is shockingly past your bedtime. I shall wait while you fetch your wrap, providing you had enough sense to bring one."

Ignoring Christina's little gasp of outrage, he turned on Levington. "You, sir, will hear from me on the morrow. For the moment, you are excused."

As he expected, both objected to this high-handed treatment. Christina he ignored. But Levington would not stand to be robbed of his treasure without a fight.

"Look here, Windermere! You cannot barge in here like this, laying claim to a lady who prefers my company to yours."

"Does she? Then, why did she first ask *me* to escort her to this kind of den? If I were you, Levington, I should learn to tell when I am being used."

"How dare you!" Christina spluttered, but Ned's accuracy had made her flush. "Go away, and let me enjoy myself. We are having a marvelous time."

Her valiant effort to cover up an all-too-obvious misery relieved Ned's tension as it brought a reluctant smile to his lips.

"It pains me to deprive you of the pleasure you were so evidently enjoying when I entered the room. Nevertheless, I fear I must."

This second proof of his perspicacity rendered Christina temporarily speechless. Fighting a betraying smile, she struggled for breath.

"You heard the lady." Levington's feeble threat was made in a low, cautious growl.

Christina's raised voice had caused a number of heads to turn their way. Soon the boxer from the door, an old sparring partner of Ned's, would come to discover the cause of the disturbance.

"This young lady"—Ned was careful not to employ Christina's name—"will be leaving under my escort. I shall see her safely home."

"Over my dead body."

At Levington's stubbornness, Ned's temper rekindled.

He took a step nearer, permitting Levington to see the fury in his gaze. The baron started back with an involuntary step but, remembering his audience, resumed a threatening pose.

"You may make as big a scene as you like." Ned spoke through a tightened jaw. "But if you do, you will find yourself the bane of polite Society. What do you suppose the duke's reaction will be if he discovers you have walked out with his sister without his permission? That alone should ruin you. But when it is discovered to what type of establishment you have brought her, an innocent lady, you will never again be received. I guarantee it."

Levington tried not to flinch under the lash of Ned's tongue, but he found it impossible not to retreat. He stammered, "I merely acceded to the lady's request. I knew it wasn't prudent for her to be seen at a house like this. That's why I arranged for the masks."

Ned nodded grimly. "I am happy to find you preserved a touch of discretion. Show more on this occasion, and I shall take her home without further ado. Our quarrel would best be left for later, if you still wish for one."

Levington's gaze had flitted to Christina's masked face and back to Ned's several times while he was listening. Now, he hesitated only a moment before making a bow. Wishing Christina good night, he made his apologies for not being able to escort her home and quickly retired.

As soon as he was gone, Ned took Christina by the arm and said, "Where is your cloak?"

Her struggles to free herself were easily foiled by the tightness of his grip. Abashed, she quit after only a few useless yanks, raising her chin as if she'd decided on her own that it was time to leave.

"I left it with the footman near the door."

"Then let's fetch it."

With no more words between them, they found her wrap and headed out of the house. Ned quickly hired them a passing vehicle and thrust her in.

Christina's pulse skipped a beat when Ned set himself beside her on the bench. She told herself it was purely from annoyance that her evening had been spoiled, but a cold nugget of dread had settled in her stomach. She knew she had driven him too far.

If Ned was not entirely disgusted by her behavior this evening, she would be very much surprised. But she had been forced by a relentless need to seek escape from her loneliness. How could he expect her to sit at home and make endless polite conversation at balls, when her heart felt as if it had a great, gaping hole in its center?

She was determined not to be the first to speak. She would never apologize for her conduct even though she knew it had been wrong.

She might have known she had no need to worry. Ned was perfectly capable of launching an attack.

His strategy, however, surprised her, as he leaned back against the side of the carriage. In a mildly curious voice, which held an undefinable current, he said, "I wonder if you could tell me why you seem so hell-bent on destroying the one possession with which a lady is blessed."

"If you mean my reputation, I would say it is because I place a much lower value on it than you do."

"That is perfectly obvious. But I find myself surprised that you would risk your security as well."

Christina felt a start. "I do not perfectly understand you."

"No? Then all the more reason for worry. Are you truly so green that you have no notion of the danger you have just escaped?"

"Escaped?" She laughed. "As I recall, I was having a perfectly splendid time until you saw fit to deprive me of an enjoyable evening."

"Let us not play games, Christina." His casual tone had vanished. "If it has fallen to me to educate you, then I shall do it, rudely or no.

"Has it not occurred to you that you put yourself entirely in the power of Lord Levington? A man who, you have been repeatedly informed, is a desperate fortune hunter who might quite logically have designs on a girl as wealthy as you. Count yourself fortunate he did not take advantage of the situation you offered him to force a condition that would make you grateful to marry him, or for Robert to pay twice any price he asked."

Christina felt all the humiliating justness of Ned's words. A sting began behind her eyelids. But she could not easily forgive him for having uttered the truth in such a way.

She would not cave in to his scolding. "You much mistake the case, my lord. Lord Levington would do nothing to harm me. I was in no danger whatsoever."

"No danger!"

She could almost hear his frustration mounting. In the dark, she could dimly see the hard-cut planes of his face.

"What you need, my dear, is an experience that will open your eyes to most men's motives."

"Oh? And what could those possibly be?"

Instead of answering her immediately, Ned gave a low, unamused laugh, a sign that she had got his goat once again. At the sound, Christina's spirits began to rise.

"Never you mind," he said grimly, "but a good, thorough kiss from one of your swains would put an end to this recklessness of yours."

"A kiss?" Despite the instant pulse that had leapt into her throat, she would not allow him to intimidate her again. "A simple kiss means nothing to me. I cannot see why you would believe such a tiny thing would frighten me."

"I'm talking about a man's kiss, my dear. Not a parent's or a nursemaid's."

Infusing boredom into her voice, Christina treated him to a condescending trill of laughter. "My dear, sweet Ned. Surely you must realize that I have been mauled before."

She felt him start up on the bench before he quickly reined his temper in. Feeling his tension coiled beside her, she could not resist one final jab.

"The drawing-master at my seminary confessed he was desperately in love with me." Ennui dripped like honey from her lips. "But his overtures were simply tiresome, not the least bit scary."

Before she could even finish this speech, Ned loomed in front of her. His silhouette blocked the light from the street. "I said a man, Christina. Not a bloody drawing-master."

With a move so smooth she barely felt it coming, he wrapped her thoroughly in his arms. His hands tangled in the hair at the nape of her neck, and with a yank, he forced her to raise her chin.

He untied her mask and slid it back from her face. When Christina gasped at the feeling of bareness, Ned wed his lips to hers.

She *had* been kissed. Or, at least, she thought she had, if the drawing-master's struggles to meet with her mouth had fulfilled the terms of a kiss. Whatever they had been, the incident had been enough to have her sent down. Only her mother's high indignation had caused her to be reinstated.

But those clumsy fumblings had held nothing like this. No unerring aim to invade her mouth with the flavor of excitement; no warmth from his lips to heat her own, carrying fire all the way to her toes; no increasing tenderness to make the sound of his quickened breathing a melody to her ears.

Christina melted toward him. Her eyelids drifted closed, and she offered herself most willingly to the nibbles he trailed down her neck. Ned's hands, those beautiful, long-fingered hands whose strength she'd gazed at and admired, stroked her face and throat, framing his soft, burning kisses and his deepening moans with the gentleness she'd always sensed he possessed.

When he pulled away, pushing her from him abruptly, Christina issued a gasping sigh of disappointment.

Ned's voice was ragged as he said, "*That* was a kiss, my dear."

"Was it?" She couldn't hide a dreamy note. "I shouldn't call that frightening."

"No?" There was a hint of pain in his tone. "Perhaps I should have been less the gentleman then."

Turning sharply from her, Ned called up to the driver to stop. Christina saw, then, that they had arrived at the corner of Grosvenor Square. Ned's irritation had shaken her out of her fog. Cold despair settled in.

"If my kiss didn't frighten you," he said through gritted teeth, "you might try imagining Levington's instead.

"Where is this window of yours?" With an abrupt change of subject, he took her by the hand and pulled her roughly after him out of the carriage. He yanked upon her cloak, drawing it closely about her unmasked face.

"What window?" She'd been knocked for a loss by the sudden alteration in his mood.

"The one you used to escape."

She raised her chin in the air and tightened her lips to stop their quivering. "I did not climb out of a window. My maid helped me out. She will be waiting to let me in by the pantry door."

"Bribed her, did you? I should have thought as much."

"No." Christina bit back. "She is devoted to me."

"Then, I shall have to pity her."

It was cold in the street without the slightest hint of daylight to warm it, but Christina's shaking had begun in Ned's arms and it wouldn't stop. Her teeth were chattering. If not with fear, then with something much more alarming.

"You may leave me here. I do not require your assistance." Her insolent manner was meant to punish him for getting her into this state, then treating her like such a brute.

But Ned was so intent upon returning her to the house, he did not seem to notice her slighting tone as he led her around through the mews.

"Hush!" he threw back over his shoulder.

Fuming, Christina nevertheless minded her tongue. She knew as well as he what Robert would think if he found them out together at this hour of the night. He would never forgive either of them, and he would quite likely make them marry. As if she would go along with such a disgusting idea!

The rear door stood in complete darkness. Christina swept past Ned and made a light scratching sound on the panel near her ear.

There followed the sounds of a scraping chair leg, a quick, light step, and the clunk of a bolt being opened with a soft cry of relief, and then Mary's face appeared in the opening, cast in light by the candle in her hand.

"Thank goodness you've come 'ome, milady!"

"Does my brother know I've been gone?"

"No, milady. They 'aven't come in yet. I was just that worried!"

"There was no need, Mary, as I told you."

While Christina had been greeting her maid, Ned had remained with one foot on the threshold.

Now he gave a snort. "You would serve your mistress better, Mary, if you refused to help her in these escapades."

The maid gave a bobbing curtsy. Her whisper rose on a wail. "And don't I know it, my lord. But 'tis all I can do to see she dresses like a Christian and not one of them heathenish statues. I see you took care of her, my lord."

"I did, indeed."

There was no understanding the exact timbre of Ned's last words, but Christina felt a leap in her heart at the thought of what had passed between them in the carriage. Her face felt as if it had been scrubbed with sand, and she wondered if her lips looked as burned as they felt.

Fortunately, to keep from attracting the other servants' attention, Mary had lit only one candle, and a small one at that.

"That will be enough now, Mary. You may run along to bed."

"We will all go to bed," Ned declared. "Mary, I charge you to lock this door and not let your mistress out again."

To Christina, it seemed he was avoiding her gaze. Some of his irritation had vanished during this interlude with Mary. If not for his rage, the scene would have had such a domestic quality, as if Ned and she had returned home together after an evening out. If they had been Robert and Louisa, they might now have gone up the stairs together to drop in on Robert Edward before seeking each other's warmth in bed.

But Ned stepped back outside without so much as a good-night. "Make sure your mistress stays in her room until morning," he threw back over his shoulder to Mary. And then he was gone.

Christina went tiredly upstairs to bed. She let Mary help her out of her clothes and tuck her under the covers. She did not know whether to be joyous that she had finally goaded Ned into noticing she was no longer the schoolgirl he thought, or heartsick because the knowledge seemed to mean so little to him.

Chapter Seven

*S*he stayed abed the next morning and only made it down to breakfast at noon. She was listlessly picking over a selection of meats and fish when Louisa joined her, bearing Robert Edward in her arms.

"There you are, my dear," she said, examining Christina's pale complexion with a mildly worried frown. "I hope your headache is not still bothering you."

"Headache?" With Ned's kisses so fresh in her mind, Christina had forgotten her excuse of the previous evening. "Oh, yes, headache! No, Louisa, I am quite well, thank you. Perhaps a bit worn. That is all."

"Thank goodness. Although you must tell me at once if it returns, and I shall call our excellent Dr. Gardiner out to see you."

"I don't think that will be necessary." Grateful for her sister-in-law's solicitude, Christina managed a smile but was afraid it must appear a trifle wan. "If you had told me a few weeks ago that I could be exhausted by a continuous round of parties, I should not have believed you."

"We are all a bit weary," Louisa conceded as she took a chair across the table. Smiling and cooing at the baby facing her on her lap, she bounced him while they talked.

"Perhaps you would rather stay at home this evening. I am certain Robert, at least, would be grateful for the rest.

And your own ball will soon be taking place. You must not let yourself become prostrated by so much gaity."

Christina considered Louisa's proposal. The prospect of an evening in which she would not have to pretend to be happy dancing with other men—when Ned refused to partner her—was tempting, she had to admit. But if she stayed at home, then he might think she had shied away because of his kiss. Christina could not let him believe he had frightened her, any more than she wanted him to think she was in love with him. She refused to be in love with Ned, for he was a confirmed bachelor. No rogue like Ned would be tempted to marry an innocent like her.

Over and over again during the night, she had revisited that scene in the carriage. She wondered if she'd imagined Ned's increasing passion the longer his caresses had continued. There was nothing in her own experience to make her certain, but it had seemed he was not entirely composed. And the possibility that he had not been unaffected by their embrace gave her the courage to rise once again to the fight.

Realizing that Louisa was awaiting her response, she quickly said, "Oh, I think I shall rally before this evening. I have already had one night's repose." Then, the notion that Louisa and Robert might prefer to stay at home struck her. "However, if you and Robert have had more than you can bear, you must say."

"Me? No." Louisa laughed and bounced her little marquess higher on her knee. "So long as we go out after Robert Edward goes to bed, I am perfectly happy. I have been quite entertained this Season, watching all the young men flock about you."

"Have you?" Christina asked, for some reason not so well pleased by Louisa's revelation. She added wryly, "I am happy to have supplied you with a diversion."

"I am not the only one who is benefiting from your coming-out."

"No?" Christina gave her head a tilt. "I cannot believe you mean Robert. I have heard him complain loudly enough."

"No, I am sorry for it, of course, but I do not mean Robert. It was Ned I was thinking of."

"Ned?" Christina's heart gave a little jump.

"Yes, indeed." Louisa turned the baby around to let him face Christina and, spying her, Robert Edward broke out in an engaging, toothless grin. "Since you came, Ned has spent so many evenings watching over you, he has had no time for his former pursuits."

"Since I came?" Christina tried to hide her avid curiosity by picking up her fork and moving the food about on her plate, but her hand was trembling. "And what pursuits would those be?"

Louisa gave her a speaking glance. "I am sure that Robert would not wish me to mention such goings-on to you, but you are already aware that Ned was the greatest rake in London. When I say his former pursuits, I am speaking of *those* sorts of activities."

"You mean drinking and gambling and . . ."

"So forth," Louisa agreed. "You know exactly to what I was referring."

"And you say he has given those up?"

"Well, not entirely perhaps, although it is many weeks since I have heard a woman's name paired with his. And you cannot deny he has remained sober, for we have seen him nearly every evening until quite late, and there has never been so much as a sign of inebriation. He might have played at cards," she admitted, "but I am certain we should have heard of any extraordinary bets.

"And," Louisa added with a great, relieved sigh, "I

have yet to hear that he has risked his neck on any athletic feat this Season."

"But why should my coming have had any effect on him whatsoever?"

Louisa shrugged and widened her eyes. "Why, indeed?"

Christina felt a lightening in her chest along with a burgeoning sense of worth, before the lessons of a lifetime reminded her how foolish self-indulgent thoughts could be. "Perhaps," she said, affecting indifference, though she longed for Louisa to contradict her, "Ned is taking his vows as godfather more seriously than we ever believed he would."

"I had not thought of that." Louisa frowned lightly as if considering, then briskly shook her head. "I suppose that could be; however, if that were the case, I should think his visits to Robert Edward would have increased. Instead, according to Nurse, he is sneaking into the nursery far less often. With the Season started, I do not think he has had as much time to come.

"And yet," she added, "he has managed to attend every function we've been invited to so far."

A vast sigh accompanied these last words. As Christina stared at her, wondering what she meant to imply, Louisa darted a few uneasy glances her way.

"What?" Christina asked, determined to know what was in her sister-in-law's mind.

Reluctance, alternating with regret, moved across Louisa's face. "If you promise not to refine too much upon what I say . . ."

"Of course. You have my word."

"It is Ned." As Louisa spoke his name, a tragic look came into her eyes.

"What? What has happened?"

"Nothing yet. But I cannot help the feeling that something might. And then where would we be?"

"We?"

"Yes, you, Robert, and I, although it would be folly on my part to place any of the blame on you, as if you could prevent such a thing from happening. And as for Robert! Robert would be beside himself if he had the faintest notion."

"Notion of what?"

Pulling Robert Edward closer to her body, Louisa looked at her sadly. "I am so afraid that Ned might have developed a *tendre* for you. You know how I wished for something of the kind. But now that Robert has made himself quite clear on the subject, I should so hate to see Ned disappointed."

A nervous bubble leapt into Christina's throat. She gave a hiccuping laugh. "Whatever makes you think such an unlikely thing has occurred?"

"I don't know." Louisa glanced at her sideways from under her lashes, once and then again. "Perhaps I am only imagining things. But it does seem to me . . ."

Christina held her breath, but Louisa did not finish, and Christina did not see how she could call the conversation back.

"But whether my intuition is right or not," Louisa said, avoiding her gaze, "something tells me that Ned's feelings might be injured. And I would never like to see that happen. He does have feelings, you know, however much he tries to hide them."

The sound of a bell interrupted their talk. Startled out of her avid state, Christina thought she might scream. She jumped up and ran to the window to see who was calling and found one of her many admirers down below, with a posy in his hand.

"Oh, dear! It's Sir Anthony Bligh, and I don't wish to see him."

"Don't you, my dear? I am terribly sorry, for I thought you would, and so I told him last night." As if in response to the desperation on Christina's face, Louisa jumped up from her chair. "But you mustn't receive him if you do not wish. I shall simply tell him you still have the headache.

"Here," Louisa said, pushing the baby into Christina's arms. "Take him through the kitchen up to Nurse, and if you would not mind, you could take him out into the gardens for some air. It is such a fine day."

Quickly, she bundled them off through the rear door of the dining parlor just before their caller was admitted through the front.

Torn so rapidly from her musings, and feeling shaken, Christina made her way to the nursery with the baby in her arms. His soft little body and his warmth acted like a tonic. She felt her restless pulse start to relax.

It took more than a few minutes to make certain Robert Edward was sufficiently clothed for the out-of-doors. While Nurse held him, Christina put on her own pelisse and bonnet, all the while itching to ask Dobbs when Ned had been around last to see the baby. The thought that he might have halted his visits because she'd caught him had occurred to her, and it was with a sense of deep regret that she pondered the possibility.

Finally, as Dobbs was handing her charge over with admonitions on how to keep him warm should a sudden wind blow up, Christina simply asked, "Has Lord Windermere been up to see my nephew recently?"

"Sure and he has, milady. He came around just t'other day when your ladyship and Her Grace had gone out shopping. But I haven't seen him as much as before, for all that."

Christina barely acknowledged her answer—not knowing what to make of it in any case—but instead occupied herself with folding the baby's covers tightly about him. Lord Robert Edward was growing, and his baby swaddlings were getting too short for his lengthening frame. His kicks were getting stronger, too, which made keeping his covers in any kind of order increasingly hard.

Christina headed out the back door into the small, walled area that served as a London garden. With her thoughts half on Ned and half on the baby's expressions of wonder, she strolled up and down until exercise and the chill of the spring day brought the roses back into her cheeks.

Ned had walked through the mews, hoping to be admitted by a servant without being remarked by anyone in the family. He'd begun to feel as if a visit to Little Ned was in order.

As soon as he spied Christina, however, he ducked behind the wall and carefully watched to see what she was doing. From his vantage point, he could not hear what she was crooning to the baby, but he could see the blush of wind on her cheeks. He could also see the ripeness covering her youthful frame, the wisps of soft flaxen hair that escaped her bonnet to fly about her face, the gentle sweep of her light-colored lashes, and the sweetness of the lips that had rocked the very foundation of his senses.

Things had not gone as he had planned. He had never anticipated allowing himself to be swept away by a kiss. If he had thought at all—and clearly he had not considered his actions enough—he would have said that his intent last night had been to frighten Christina out of her wits by showing her once and for all the danger of inciting a man's hunger. He might even have momentarily believed it would be smart to let his arousal carry him away in the interest of convincing her.

But he had met with such delicious capitulation on her part. Her entirely unexpected reception of his kiss had fired his desire. He had not believed she would welcome him at all, much less return his embrace with such overwhelming passion, or that the taste of her lips would be so sweet.

The knowledge that she had relished his caress had shaken him badly. Christina was Robert's sister, and Robert had declared her too good for Ned.

Ned knew that she was. He knew she was an innocent, much too innocent for him, in spite of that impassioned kiss. It had taken an instant for her untrained lips to mold perfectly to his. But once they had . . .

Ned cursed himself for a fool and a cad. He had never meant to awaken this passion in her, or to let her see how rapidly his own desire could mount. And it had not mounted that rapidly since his first inkling of the pleasures of the flesh.

Another reason to be on guard.

Waiting for Christina to turn in the opposite direction, Ned tried to pull his gaze away from the tempting picture she made. He decided he ought to go back the way he had come. The less he saw of Christina from now on, the better things would be. He had obviously allowed himself to develop an attraction to her without realizing how fast his feelings were growing. But this, too, would pass, as had all his other *tendres*. He had only to let his passion cool.

It had been odd, now he thought of it, that Louisa had known that an affair between him and Christina was even possible. She could never have foreseen how it would grow. From complete indifference, proceeding through open hostility, they had somehow emerged as friends.

Each had something of the other's restless feeling. That shared impatience and discontent with life had led them both to commit indiscretions that set them apart from the rest of the polite world.

Only Christina had not yet revealed this inclination in such a way as to set herself beyond the realm of acceptable Society. No matter how hard she had tried.

Staring after her once again and watching her alone with the baby, Ned admitted to himself that when he was not furious with her, he could almost think he understood her. That should be no basis, however, for this lust he felt that stirred his loins even as he watched her walk. He told himself he would have found anyone with her face, hair, and girlish figure tempting. He must not let himself make more of last night's incident than there was.

Unfortunately, with her sweet, tender form pressed to his, he had forgotten that his object had been to tame her. By his very act, he had led her into the sort of behavior he had been working so hard to help her avoid. He would have to exercise more restraint. Perhaps he should even apologize.

Or maybe it would be best simply to forget that delicious kiss had ever occurred.

Ned struggled with the difficulty of this strategy. He would make himself forget. The fact that the mere sight of Christina had stirred his yearnings would soon be overcome. It might, perhaps, be easier to forget what had passed between them, if he never saw her again.

But how was that to be accomplished, when he had spent nearly all his evenings this past month in the company of her family? He could not eschew Robert and Louisa as if they were not his friends. If he did, Robert would surely begin to suspect this sudden alteration.

Worse yet, Christina herself would undoubtedly think he had shied away because the kiss had disturbed him more than it should. He could not allow her to believe in such a fantasy.

With a grim sort of stiffness gripping his innards, Ned realized he would have to carry on as before, else the chit would develop the harebrained notion that he was falling in love with her. And he could not be falling in love with such a tender girl, who could do so much better for herself than to marry a rogue.

Just as Ned was moving to go with an unwonted heaviness of heart, Christina completed a length of the garden and turned. His shadow must have caught her eye, for she halted in her tracks. He thought he heard her gasp.

Discovered, Ned could do nothing but pretend he had just arrived.

An uncommon nervousness made him swallow, as he noted the startled light in her eyes.

"Taking the air, I see." As Ned moved out from behind the wall and strolled through the gate, he spoke as if nothing extraordinary had passed between them.

Aware that she had been holding her breath, Christina responded in kind. She raised the baby and bounced him before her face to cloak her shaken expression. "Yes, we were," she said, "but you startled me. I am not terribly used to seeing men lurking behind the house. Fortunately, Robert Edward is never frightened by marauders."

"I wasn't lurking." Ned's lips gave a twist in response to her remark. "I make it a practice never to lurk."

"Call it what you like." Trying to hide her own grin, Christina raised a shoulder and tossed her nose in the air. "But approaching a person's residence from the back seems a very havey-cavey business to me."

"So does sneaking out of it in the middle of the night. You are one to talk, my dear."

At this scarcely flattering reminder of her escapade, Christina stiffened.

"But perhaps," Ned said smoothly, "it was indelicate of me to mention that particular incident. I shall endeavor not to do so again. However, in exchange for my restraint, I shall expect you to exercise a similar one."

"As if I would tell anyone what happened last night!"

Ned's brows flew up. A sparkle lit his eyes. With mortification sweeping her body, Christina realized she had misunderstood his meaning.

"Oh, I never kiss and tell," he said, and his voice was so low it brought a rapid throb to her ears. "Honor among rogues, you know.

"No, my dear"—with an abruptness that startled her, he reverted to his flippant manner—"the matter to which I was referring was my unconventional habit of entering this house through the rear for the purpose of visiting my godson unannounced."

"One might wonder how you contrive to enter a house secretly with so many servants in it."

"Ah, as to that, I have my ways."

Christina threw him a chastising frown. "By that, I suppose you mean that you bribe them. Shall I tell my brother that his servants are not to be trusted?"

"Not unless you want to see them all turned out in the streets without a character. Robert's servants are all very good, Lady Chris. They know whom they can trust and whom not. Am I not a family intimate?" Ned's expression when he asked this was one of insulted innocence.

"Hmmmm." Christina would not give him the satisfaction of an answer, but her lips longed to curve.

"I am becoming an intimate to one member at least."

Her heart began to flutter, but she told herself she must not fall into his trap of double entendre again.

Adjusting the baby's coverlet more securely about him, she merely inquired, "I hope you do not mean you have been seducing Dobbs? I wouldn't have thought her your type."

Ned cocked her a glance with one brow raised, and an evil glint lodged in his eye. "Let us simply say that Dobbs and I have a comfortable understanding."

His old roguish look was back. It struck dismay into Christina's heart. He seemed so delighted to be suspected of the worst possible wickedness.

And, suddenly, she knew why his look distressed her so. He wanted her to know how little his kisses had meant.

Their lively encounter had lost its charm. Robert Edward felt heavy in her arms.

Ned must have noticed her sagging, for he offered to carry the baby, although he managed to hide his solicitude beneath more teasing.

"Are you going to allow me a visit with my godchild or not?" he complained, reaching out with both hands. "I have been as patient as I know how to be."

At any other time, Christina might have prolonged their little game, but now, exhausted by her feelings, she merely acquiesced. Whether Ned had meant to warn her against caring for him or not, she had no wish to come between him and the baby. She knew what comfort Robert Edward could bring, and something told her that Ned needed him just as much as she.

Nothing should have kept her from going inside at that moment, but instead, she strolled up and down, watching Ned lure chuckles from the baby, wondering with a heart full of pain whether he would ever father children of his own.

* * *

Up in her room after Sir Anthony's brief visit, Louisa gazed down on the pair from her window and pensively chewed her bottom lip.

She had spied Ned as soon as he had approached the gate from the mews and with a growing sense of dismay had noted his hesitation. When he had nearly gone away, it had taken all her restraint not to open the casement and call out to him to stop.

It did not take a genius to see that something had passed between these two, which both were at pains to ignore. Christina's smiles were brilliant when they fell upon any gentleman other than Ned. The casual glances Ned threw her way betrayed nothing but an arrogant boredom. It was only when neither thought the other was watching that Louisa was able to spy the feelings they tried so hard to hide.

Louisa's instincts had told her they would be a perfect match. What Ned had needed was a woman who would keep him too busy to get up to his own mischief. He needed someone to keep him on his toes, someone for whom to be responsible, until he could forget the misdemeanors of his past and begin to see himself in a new light.

His enchantment with her baby had told Louisa how much he longed to have a family of his own to love and protect. The trouble was that most girls' parents felt the need to guard their daughters from *him*, with the result that Ned had no one looking to him for protection.

Robert's admission that Christina posed a challenge too great for one man had given Ned the excuse he needed to form an attachment. That he had been attracted to Christina from the start had been evident from that first day in the abbey, for Louisa had never seen him so out of sorts. And she had not failed to notice Christina's flutterings the first time Ned's name had been raised. Who better to appeal to a clever hoyden than a rogue who could match her every step? But two such sadly muddled beings could never be left alone to discover their fate.

Now, it seemed that something had happened to put Ned, at least, on guard against his feelings. Something the previous night, when he had brought Christina home. Christina had been so affected by whatever it was, she had almost betrayed herself this morning, unaware that Louisa's maid had already carried her the tale.

Their affair was at a critical stage. One wrong step or an ill-timed shove could destroy their only chance at happiness. The hint of opposition, an inkling of suspicion that they were being manipulated by Louisa, or even a quirk in either's personality could cause a major breach.

Nurse's tip, about the hour Ned could usually be expected to visit Robert Edward, had paid off today. At least, the two were speaking, even if every posture or gesture revealed their nervous restraint.

Christina's own ball was approaching. Louisa could only hope that the sight of Christina in her most beautiful gown, surrounded by scores of admirers, would make Ned forget his tarnished reputation long enough to declare his heart.

Chapter Eight

*A*ccording to the daily journals, Christina's ball was to be the most talked-about event of the Season. Invitations had made their way across London to more than four hundred illustrious guests: Society's grandes dames, the government's most prominent lords and ministers, as well as fashionable wits and famous men of letters. Among this number was the Prince Regent, who, according to his nearest intimates, planned to make a late appearance.

Her Grace of Broughton had spared no expense on either the lavish decorations or the tastiest refreshments to charm her company. The walls of the drawing room and dining parlor had been draped with fine layers of gauze and decked with garlands of fresh spring blooms to represent a faerie dell, while hundreds of candles added sparkle to the magical illusion.

A horde of servants had been taken on in addition to the not-inconsiderable staff of Broughton House to bring this wonder about. They glided through the packed, glittering rooms, dispensing champagne of good vintage and serving a delectable array of canapés from trays.

As Ned entered the drawing room that night, long after the receiving line had dispersed, he saw that the gossipmongers had been right. Judging by the crush of bodies through which he'd made his way, no one of any note had refused Louisa's summons. The only clear spots on the floor were those that intermittently appeared between the dancing pairs, as each abandoned one position in favor of another in accordance with the steps.

Determined as he was not to show any partiality for Christina beyond the courtesy due the guest of honor, Ned found that his eagerness to see her could not be quelled. He searched the room until he saw her, weaving through the set on her partner's arm. . . .

And took a deep, hasty breath.

Just as the walls had been adorned to resemble a woodland fantasy, Christina herself had been dressed as a faerie queen. Her fine, flaxen hair lay in a soft fringe about her face, with the rest left down to sweep her shoulders. It gleamed like gold in the light from the candles. Her skin, as fair and delicate as parchment, reflected the hazy, warm glow from the chandeliers.

As Ned stood, watching the play of light and shadow across her cheeks, the curve of her downcast lids, and the fragility of her smile, something inside him turned over.

Abruptly, he wrenched away and, stopping a passing servant, helped himself to champagne. He would not have to mount guard over Christina this evening. Broughton House had been constructed with no terrace, and the garden had no high shrubbery in which a couple might lose themselves. With such a lively throng inside, there would be no alcoves in which to hide.

Ned strolled about the room, greeting acquaintances and pausing now and then to talk, while a swirling agitation churned inside. He yearned for just one waltz with Christina, though he was certain all her dances would have been claimed. He had purposely arrived too late to face that temptation, but it had hounded him all the distance between his house and here. And now he cursed himself for spoiling his one chance.

Tonight was Christina's ball. Surely, as an old friend

of her brother's, he might have been allowed one waltz without causing tongues to wag.

Lost in these musings, Ned was startled by Louisa's voice at his side.

"Does she not look divine?"

He had not realized he'd been staring at Christina again. Caught, he did his best to sound nonchalant. "She does. You have done quite well by her, Louisa."

Her worried sigh alarmed him. "I do so hope you are right. But I cannot be happy with Robert's plans."

"Oh?" Ned feigned a humor he did not feel. "Has he found a new Buffington to woo her?"

"Yes, although I should be happier if the gentleman *were* Lord Buffington. Robert has decided that Christina needs an older man to govern her."

"Perhaps he's right." With a half-shrug, he turned and saw Louisa gazing sadly at him.

"Not you, too?" she said, disappointment in the slow shake of her head. "I had counted you among her friends."

Ned dropped his glance to the glass in his hand. He tossed it back before discovering it was empty. "Why shouldn't she marry an older man?"

"Someone who is not of her own choosing? She would be miserable."

"So, Robert has chosen her a husband?"

"I think he has. He has become impatient with her for refusing so many offers."

Ned's hand suddenly shook. "How many have there been?"

"Quite a number. And several of those from eligible gentlemen. But Christina still fails to show a decided partiality for any one of her suitors. Although . . ." With a guilty glance his way, followed by a puzzled frown, Louisa cut off her speech.

"Although . . . ," he prompted.

Fumbling nervously with the lace between her breasts, Louisa avoided his eyes. Ned fixed them firmly on her face, until she gave up with a sigh.

"If you *must* know, I think she might have developed a *tendre* for someone, but I cannot say who."

Ned's heart gave a jerk, but he concealed it with a smile. "Cannot or will not?"

"I do not know his name. And I will not pry into Christina's confidence."

The smile abandoned him. "It is just as well. He is quite likely to be unsuitable."

Louisa straightened, tilting her nose in the air. "I am not so doubtful of her judgment. If she has determined that only one man can make her happy, I am certain she is right, and I cannot bear the thought of her being wed to someone for whom she can only feel disgust."

A sickening wave roiled up inside him. "Robert would never force her into such a match."

"No. But he can bring such pressure to bear that she will decide to submit to his wishes rather than be an endless burden to her brother."

"You are being nonsensical."

"I am not! That is how women think."

A rush of pure male irritation made Ned snarl, "But why would Christina be so stupid?"

To his surprise, a glimmer of tears came into Louisa's eyes. "If the gentleman she loves does not declare himself, what other choice will she have?"

A sudden fear seized his heart. He had never imagined Christina's future. He had been far too busy guarding her reputation from willful indiscretion ever to give her future a thought. He had regarded her marriage as the successful end of the Season, even though he, along with Robert, had failed to think of any candidate for her hand who possessed just the right combination of dignity and experience.

Now he realized how short his sight had been. Christina would need more than just a guardian. She would need a companion for life, someone to laugh and make love with. Someone to share her pride in their children. Someone to hold her through misfortune and to cuddle with her on cold winter nights.

Someone to make her happy.

Louisa's comment, that she suspected Christina of having developed feelings for an undisclosed gentleman, had made him wonder if the man could be himself. Surely, if he was the first to have tapped into her passion—and he was almost certain he was—it would not be too terribly surprising if a girl her age had mistaken such passion for love.

Ned fought the triumph that threatened to burgeon inside him. He knew it was shame he should be feeling. Shame for distracting her from the very serious business of finding a suitable husband.

If he *was* the man who was keeping her from choosing a worthy mate, he had only one choice of action. He must prevent her from marrying anyone else until her preference could naturally shift to a gentleman more deserving of her love.

"I'll talk to Robert," he blurted, as much to himself as to Louisa. "He mustn't be allowed to bully her. She'll make a decent choice in time."

"I am sure she will," Louisa said, her tears vanishing in the wake of a radiant smile. "I knew I could count on you, Ned. You are always so dependable."

Her choice of word startled him. He had been called

many things before, but dependability had never been numbered among his better known virtues.

Louisa's mistake brought a cynical smile to his lips.

"You must be thinking of someone else. However, in this instance, I shall do my best."

He strolled the room and found Robert in converse with one of his guests, the sight of whom made Ned halt in his tracks.

Lord Musgrove. Tall, frail, and obliged by his thinning hair to wear a wig, he was the son of the aged Duke of Gilmorgan. A marquess, in his fifties if he was a day, he had a pronounced disdain for frivolous Society. Not yet come into his main inheritance, he seldom ventured into London; but rumor had it that the duke could not possibly last much longer, so Lord Musgrove was finally on the lookout for a wife.

Anger swelled in Ned. If this was the man Robert had selected for Christina, he would have something blunt to say.

Christina had long since given up hope that Ned would invite her to dance. His tardy arrival had resulted in the effect of an icy bath. She felt chilled to the bone, and no number of compliments or amount of flattering attention from other men could raise a warmth in her veins.

Feeling pale and thin in all her responses, she had nevertheless done her best to live up to the honor Robert and Louisa had done her by giving this ball. She had been generous with her smiles and had danced with every gentleman who'd been presented to her. The only privilege she had reserved for herself had been the choice of her supper partner.

She had delayed her decision until a real danger loomed of being forced to accept Lord Musgrove, Robert's current favorite. She had decided Lord Levington would squire her.

He had been invited despite Robert's wishes. Louisa had been adamant that a man who had rendered her such a service in the park could not be ignored.

Now, as Christina walked into the parlor where chairs had been set up for supper, she felt as if she might as well endure the penance of Levington's company. Her experience with Ned had proven how unappealing she was to anyone who could inspire her devotion. Despite his passionate kisses, Ned had obviously decided she was unworthy of more.

Levington secured a pair of chairs and signaled to a footman to supply them with plates, then to another to fill Christina's glass with champagne. He seemed pleased when she immediately raised it to her lips.

The strong, fizzing liquid stung her throat and nose, but her second sip went down much more smoothly and brought a sudden heat to her cheeks. The third left her with a warm, syrupy lassitude that partially chased away her rebellious spirits.

"I had almost feared I would not be invited this evening." With a knowing smile, Levington leaned across his chair until his head was mere inches away from hers.

"Oh? And why was that, my lord?"

"I had begun to think your brother did not approve of me."

"Undoubtedly, he does not."

The champagne had added a certain directness to her speech. Levington's evident dismay raised a giggle in Christina's throat, but she smothered it.

"It is the duchess, then, who invited me?"

"She and I drafted most of the list."

His smugness returned, taking shape in that slow, intimate smile. "Then here we are at last."

A wave of self-disgust nearly overcame her. Christina lowered her gaze to her plate and toyed with her food. Until this moment, she had not considered how her choice of dinner partner at her own ball might be viewed, especially by that choice.

Levington bent to whisper in her ear. "Will you give me leave to speak to your brother tomorrow?"

"I doubt you should make the attempt. Robert has not been known to express kindly feelings toward you."

He pulled back quickly, a scowl on his face, before he attempted to recover his good humor.

He moved nearer again, and his voice was low. "Are you saying we would do best to marry without his notice?"

"I have never said I would marry you, my lord." Christina turned sharply toward him, so that he might see her sincerity.

An angry light came into his eyes.

"My dear Lady Christina, surely you have intimated as much by your encouragement of my attentions. And I see no need for qualms as long as the duchess favors my suit, which I believe she does."

"You are gravely mistaken. Louisa will accept my wishes with respect to my own future happiness."

Lord Levington's gaze narrowed to a slit as he slowly sat back in his chair.

Christina felt her own stare wavering as the error she had made burst fully upon her. With all the fortitude she possessed, she reminded herself that this man had wanted her for her fortune alone.

"It seems in that case that I have made a mistake," he said with a sneer. "I had thought my attentions more agreeable to you. If you have no objection, I shall take myself off."

"I give you leave."

As he rose from his seat, Christina kept her eyes downcast. All around her, guests grouped together in twos and threes were enjoying the delicious fare. The din in the parlor was such that no one could have heard what had passed between them.

When Levington had gone, she stayed where she was only long enough to make certain she would not run into him, but not long enough for someone to wonder that her partner had not returned. Exhausted in spirit and body, she quietly rose as if intending to rejoin the dance.

Instead, she made her way to the rear of the house where a servants' staircase took her up to the second floor. She hoped her absence would not be noticed before she could collect herself again.

Once within the privacy of her own room, she removed her gloves and sat down on the bed. She could not recline without wrinkling her dress, so she simply closed her eyes and let despair roll through her.

She had defied the conventions. She had run all the risks her restless mind had forced her to run. And still she had not been happy. Sometimes she wondered if it would take utter ruin to quash this discontent that drove her on.

She remembered Ned's warning, that social ruin would not bring her joy, and in her heart she believed him. Why, then, could she not stop herself from pursuing that very object?

The door to her room gave a click. She opened her eyes and jumped when she saw Ned filling the doorway. His angry expression chased the blood from her cheeks.

After a few moments, he silently closed the door behind him, before turning to lean against the casement with his arms crossed. Seeing him there when she had believed he had forgotten her made her heart beat queerly.

She was unprepared for his first words. "Levington is

not yet here, I see. We shall be able to scotch this scandal before it takes place."

"Lord Levington?" Christina was taken aback, but the scorn in his voice had flicked her like a whip. "Whatever can you mean?"

A slow, hard smile formed on his lips, but it did not warm his eyes. "I saw him leave the dining parlor. Then, after a discreet interval, you also left. I have to credit you, Lady Chris. Not many girls would have the gall to seduce their escort at their own ball."

Enraged beyond speech, Christina surged to her feet. With balled fists at her sides, she started to move toward him, but an angry devil inside her made her stop.

She made a half-turn with her body, so that Ned could not see her face. "So you saw us, did you? And you came up to stop me from this ultimate indiscretion. How kind of you, Ned."

Out of the corner of her eye, she saw his body go rigid. He took an involuntary step her way.

"This is no cause for jokes. What in the name of Satan could you have been thinking of to place yourself in such a compromising situation? If you want Levington, why don't you marry him and spare the people who love you so much anguish?"

Tears were forming in Christina's eyes, but she fought them down. "Is that what I should do?" she asked in a tremulous voice. "Marry Levington?"

"No!" In two quick strides, Ned crossed to her. He took her by the shoulders and spun her around. Giving her a shake so hard it rattled her teeth, he said, "That scoundrel isn't worth the tip of your finger. Anybody— take your pick—even Buffington or Musgrove would be better than Levington." He gave a derisive snort. "Even *I* would make a better husband."

With those words, Christina's eyes, which she had

squeezed tightly shut to keep her tears from falling, flew wide open. She saw a haunting desperation in his gaze, and her heart took a leap. "Are you saying I should marry you instead?"

A shocked, guilty look—full of fear and hope—broke over his face. His fingers dug deeply into her arms, and he gave a ragged gasp. Christina wished with all her might that he would embrace her. Ned seemed torn between thrusting her from him and pulling her to his chest.

"Good God!" Robert's voice surprised them both, making them spin to face the door, where he stood with an air of outraged hurt. "And to think I trusted you.

"I must have been a fool," he said, looking at Ned with disappointment and disgust. "That you would betray the confidence you have enjoyed in this house to persuade my sister into this. I never should have turned my back on you. I went against my better judgment, but I let myself be foolishly persuaded."

Christina saw that Ned had gone white, as white as a sheet of paper. Before she could utter a word in his defense, Robert drew himself up.

"I must ask you to leave." His speech admitted no room for discussion.

To Christina's dismay, Ned simply complied. His mouth twisted with irony, but he spoke not a word of explanation. Instead, he made a formal bow to Robert, before repeating his obeisance to her more slowly.

"My apologies, madam, if I have done anything to give disgust."

The complete resignation with which this was said wrung Christina's heart. For the first time, she felt Ned's deep sense of worthlessness, and it rang in such harmony with her own as to paralyze her now.

In a moment he was gone. Robert stood quietly in the room until he could conquer his anger enough to speak.

"Downstairs are four hundred guests assembled in your honor. Will you please have the goodness to grant them your company?"

Stunned by all that had occurred in the past few minutes, Christina walked numbly past him. She went downstairs, and for the rest of the night a brittle smile concealed the tumult in her mind.

Once their guests had gone, Christina exercised her remaining strength to correct Robert's misapprehension of the events. Surprisingly, the simple truth made the best story because, for once, Christina had nothing to hide.

Robert, however, was not so easy to convince. The evidence of his eyes tended to contradict what she said. Had he not discovered her alone in her bedroom with Ned? And had Ned not put his arms about her?

No matter how many times Christina informed him with increasing asperity that Ned had made the same mistake as he, but that his particular mode of punishment had been to try to shake the teeth from her head, Robert would not bend. He conceded that her own behavior might have been innocent. But if Ned's had been, why had he refused to contradict the charges?

Christina could not answer this question without delving into facets of her own character she was only now beginning to understand. And though she could not be certain that the hurts she had experienced could be applied equally to Ned, she thought they might.

When one has been accused from one's infancy of evil intent, it is somehow easier to be the person one is imagined to be than to continue trying to prove that others are wrong.

That Ned had been severely hurt was obvious. His

face, when Robert had accused him of the worst sort of treachery, throwing in doubt all their friendship had meant, was a sight Christina hoped never to see again. But perhaps his own confusion over his motives had contributed to an appearance of guilt.

He *had* kissed her in the carriage. Had he meant to embrace her again last night before they'd been interrupted?

Whatever the case, she would never know. Robert stated in no uncertain terms that thenceforth she was never to see Ned again.

It was a miserable party that climbed the stairs of Broughton House to seek their rooms at dawn. Louisa put an arm about Christina's waist and urged her to bed. She promised they would talk after they had all got some rest.

As Louisa had feared, the worst had happened. Somehow, she trusted Christina's version of the story.

More alert to her sister-in-law's doings than either gentleman knew, Louisa had not failed to notice when Lord Levington left the ball. She had not witnessed Christina's trip upstairs; but knowing the watch Ned had always kept upon her movements, the number of times he had forestalled her most wanton escapades, and the pitch of his feelings that night, she did not doubt he had acted, rashly perhaps, but still with Christina's better interest at heart.

Her own part in raising his level of anxiety, Louisa deplored. She had pressed him too hard and too fast when, clearly, Ned could not begin to see himself as a legitimate suitor. And now that Robert had thrown his sordid reputation in his teeth, he would be even less likely to do so.

Added to all this heartache and disappointment was Robert's anger at Louisa herself. She sighed. She had made a pig's mess of everything, and yet she absolutely must not back out now.

Both Ned and Christina deserved a chance in life, yet life had wrung all hope from both. If they were ever to come together, Louisa would have to go directly against her husband's wishes. She could not bear the thought of hurting Robert, but she must do what was right.

She only hoped that Robert would come to forgive her in time.

Chapter Nine

*N*ed stayed abed until midafternoon, sleeping off a headache from too much champagne. He could not so easily rid himself of the more nagging pain in his chest.

He was sitting in his breakfast parlor, staring with little appetite at a plate filled with ham and bacon, eggs, and pickled fish, when His Grace of Broughton was announced.

Robert abruptly entered the smallish room. The black severity of his morning costume lent an air of strain to his already pallid skin. The stiffness in his shoulders made Ned want to sigh.

Instead of rising to greet his guest in an obsequious manner, Ned pushed back in his chair and crossed his arms.

"Well, Broughton," he asked, "have you come to apologize or to call me out? If it's the latter, I should warn you my seconds have grown quite weary of transacting my affairs of late."

Robert took this as a poor attempt at humor—when, as Ned could have informed him, it was the truth.

"I have not come to call you out," Robert said irritably, "but neither am I certain you deserve any sort of apology."

"No doubt you are right." Ned unfolded his arms and, despite his lack of appetite, took up his knife and fork.

"You will not mind, I hope, if I eat before the fat on this bacon congeals?"

"Hang it, Ned! How can you eat at a time like this?"

Ned raised his brows. "Have you not breakfasted yet?"

"You know I have. I would not otherwise be out."

"Then you will understand my pressing need for sustenance." With his fork, he pointed to a chair across the table. "You may sit, if you like. That should prevent you from pacing a hole in my Turkey carpet."

Ignoring Robert's offended glance and attacking his plate with a feigned relish, Ned spoke between bites. "You might have the goodness to tell me why I am to be spared a drawing and quartering."

Seating himself with a show of reluctance, Robert gnawed on the inside of his cheek. He appeared both angry and uncertain. "Christina said you followed her to her room to break up—as you mistakenly thought—an assignation with Levington."

Ned looked up sharply. "Was I mistaken, then?"

"If her story is true, you were. She said she had merely gone to her room to rest before dancing again."

"And where was Levington?"

"Louisa said he had left. But this is not about Levington, Ned. It is about you and what you were doing when I walked in."

"I assume Christina has told you all about that, too. But you don't believe her, I see."

"How can I, when you looked as if you were about to ravish her? There, in her own room!"

"It did look black, I suppose. What does Christina have to say about it?"

Robert glanced at him guiltily. "That you got angry with her for planning an indiscretion, and so you shook her."

"Is that all she said?"

Robert sat up straighter. "What the devil do you mean?"

"I am saying"—Ned lent a harder edge to his voice—"that no matter what Christina says, you still have your doubts. You were right, and you always have been right, not to trust me, Robert. You should never have let your sister near me. Fortunately, no one but us is aware of what transpired last night, and as it was, it was nothing. But if I were you, I should prevent her from seeing anyone remotely as bad as me for the rest of her life."

His frankness took Robert's breath away. He recoiled, and his eyes searched Ned's face.

"I still don't understand you," he said, wary.

"It is very simple." Ned resumed his breakfast, though his throat was dry. "I have every respect for your sister. However, as you must have told yourself a hundred times, she can only be harmed by any intimacy with me. You yourself jumped to the wrong conclusion last night. If we had been discovered by anyone else, that person or persons would have been much less forgiving."

Robert was staring at him, still bemused.

Ned wiped his mouth with a serviette and put it down before leaning back again. "What have I said to confuse you?" he asked.

"I don't know," Robert responded with a frown. "But you have to admit it's deuced odd."

"What is?" In spite of the leaden weight that had seemed to press down upon his chest since yesterday evening, Ned's affection for Robert made him smile.

"The way you sounded so serious. Why would you warn me against yourself? There must be a trick in it somewhere."

Ned felt his smile fade. A bitter grimace took its place. "Undoubtedly, there must. However, since I have only given you a confirmation of what you already know,

I should not waste too much time stewing over it, if I were you.

"Look," he added, feeling the need to remove himself from a scene in which he could only play the villain, "if it would make you feel any more secure with respect to Christina, I shall take myself off. I could stand a few weeks in the country. And I could even take Levington with me for a spell. He could use the break from his creditors' calls, and you would be getting rid of both of us at once."

Robert must have noticed the bitterness Ned had tried so hard to suppress. "I doubt that will be necessary," he said, looking ashamed.

To Ned, however, it seemed that his protest was less than sincere. "It will be no trouble at all. I do have one request, however, if you are willing."

"What is that?" Robert seemed to brace himself for the trick he suspected.

Ned grinned without any mirth. "I should like to pay a visit to Robert Edward and Louisa before I go. I promise not to see Christina."

A slight hesitation on Robert's part was enough to cause a tightening sensation in Ned's throat. But, he reflected, he should not have been surprised. Robert's lack of faith was no more than he deserved.

He had subverted Robert's servants to gain entry to his house. He had concealed Christina's most wanton behavior from her brother and guardian. He had betrayed Robert's trust by giving in—once, and nearly a second time last night—to his lustful feelings for Robert's sister. He deserved to be mistrusted for all the things he'd done even though he had never meant any harm.

But that had always been his way. He had always been heedless and careless, and he'd discovered his errors too late to repair them. That was why he was considered such a rogue.

"But, perhaps"—Ned filled the silence himself—"you prefer not to trust me in the house with your wife."

Robert's frown held shock and more than a hint of chagrin. "Don't be such a complete ass, Ned. I wasn't thinking about that. I was merely trying to come up with the proper time for your visit. Would Tuesday afternoon suit?"

"Certainly." Ned hid his immense relief. He was not to be cut off from Robert's family entirely. "If he agrees to go with me, Levington and I could take off the next day for Yorkshire."

"You don't have to do that, you know. I did not ask it of you."

In response, Ned stood, giving Robert a stiff nod. But he said nothing beyond sending his compliments to Louisa with a request to see her on Tuesday next.

When Robert left, Ned sat down again, but he could not eat.

There, he thought. He had done what was best for Christina. He had nearly fooled himself into thinking he could resist her and still watch over her, but last night had proven him wrong.

How he had been so impulsive as to follow her to her room in defiance of every prudent thought, he did not know, but the sight of her rising only moments after Levington had fired his suspicions. He had thought her over Levington, but when he had seen them whispering so intimately, he had let jealousy get the most of his sense.

And in his anger over her foolishness, he had made the mistake of touching her again, and for a moment he had looked into her eyes. The invitation he had seen there had made him want to give in to a host of yearnings he had not known he possessed.

145

A desire for a home. A painful need to be tender. And a wish for someone other than himself to love.

It was good, he convinced himself now, that Robert had interfered in time to remind him of how unfit he was even to dream of quenching his desires in Christina's arms.

From this moment, his only task would be to leave her alone, to hide this still burning wish to hold her, so the world at large would never know how close Christina had come to being ravished by a rogue. He would have to trust Robert to keep her henceforth out of trouble. But, just in case, Ned would make good on his promise to get Levington out of the way.

Louisa had failed to persuade Robert to change his mind. She could not use her normal clever tactics when her husband was so distressed. In spite of Christina's revelations, he had seen enough to convince him that Ned's feelings for his sister could no longer be considered in an avuncular light and no others from such a quarter would be acceptable.

And now Ned had added his own bit of foolishness to the equation by deciding to be noble.

Though sympathetic, Louisa had a strong desire to wring his neck.

She was equally exasperated with her husband for failing to see how ideally suited the two were. And with Christina for being too afraid of having her love spurned to declare it.

Which she was.

So deep in misery that she had no idea how much it showed, Christina had taken the tack that Robert's high-handed pronouncement was nothing more than a bit of silliness, which he would soon forget, but which in the interim scarcely affected her at all. The only regret she'd confessed was that Robert and Ned should have had a falling out over such an insignificant incident.

On the contrary, Louisa opined, Robert and Ned were all too much in accord. Robert had declared his friend a scoundrel, and Ned had seconded the motion.

Ned appeared on Tuesday, as agreed. He saluted Louisa with a kiss on one cheek before demanding to hold her son.

Dimpling at his impudence, she relinquished Robert Edward to his arms, then took a chair across from Ned to examine his face.

He seemed to have sobered in the past few weeks. Where before there had always been a restless sense of energy, she now saw the result of a lack of sleep. Even his impudence had been forced. He looked more anchored, though, as if this period of relative abstinence had removed some of the agitation from his veins.

He had the look of a man ready to settle down, if not for the fact that the woman he loved had been denied him.

Louisa did not allow his attempts at joviality to fool her into thinking he had not been affected by Robert's charges. Ned might be adept at concealing his most painful emotions; but when he held Robert Edward on his knees and peered into his eyes, his mask fell away, betraying a rawness Louisa could hardly bear to watch.

With this evidence of his misery, Louisa could no longer be vexed at his foolishness. She put on a smile to cover an urge to cry.

Ned was unaware that Robert had informed her of their interview. Neither would he relish the knowledge that she was privy to his disgrace. Louisa had always displayed her faith in Ned, and she had taken pains to let him know that she regarded the worst of his escapades as nothing more than boyish pranks. As a result, Ned had confided in her more than he had in anyone else. With her, he was not so often inclined to exaggerate his wickedness.

She wished he would confide in her now, so that she might find a way to bring him back to Christina. She tried to draw him out.

"Robert tells me you have decided to leave us for a while?"

"Yes." Ned bounced Robert Edward into the air and earned a gurgling laugh that softened his expression before his mask descended again. "I thought a jaunt into the country might be amusing. A bit of fishing and shooting, perhaps. I've got a new tiger. I need to take him up into Yorkshire to introduce him to my stable there. Train him a bit. That sort of thing."

"Isn't this rather sudden?"

"No, I've been needing a new groom ever since my last one took that fall."

"Oh." Louisa felt frustrated by this clear signal that he refused to confide in her this time. She worked for a different opening. "Tell me about this boy," she said. "Where did you find him?"

"At Tattersall's. He had sneaked inside and was sleeping in a stall. They didn't have a spot for him, so I took him on."

"That was good of you, Ned."

"Nonsense. Anybody knows that the best grooms are made of boys who love to be with horses. A pure piece of selfishness on my part.

"He is still a little young, but I have some hopes for him. He shows talent. His only fault seems to be a tendency to be distracted by every passing wench. But who am I to fault him for that?" Ned grinned and arched his brows, but his attempt to amuse her at his own expense lacked any genuine sense of fun.

Louisa gave an obligatory smile, before something so outrageous it at once both shocked and delighted her leapt into her mind.

"I vow, you have made this boy sound so amusing, I should dearly love to see him," she said.

"A new cause, Louisa?"

"Not at all, when he is in such good hands. I merely wondered whether he posed a danger to my maids. But I suppose you did not bring him today."

"Indeed I did. He is supposed to be out in the square, holding my horses' heads. If you look out the window, you can judge him for yourself."

"Oh, that won't be necessary." She laughed, but silently she vowed she would get a good look at the boy without Ned's being aware. "I daresay I'll glimpse him up behind you one day.

"How will you be going into Yorkshire?" she asked.

"In my curricle. I'll take the boy to accustom him to my ways."

Louisa clasped her hands together. "Your whole trip sounds absolutely delightful. I think you are wise to get away."

Her unwarranted enthusiasm made Ned regard her with a skeptical air, but a big hiccup from Robert Edward distracted him before he could question her.

Louisa rejoiced at the opportunity.

She jumped to her feet, saying, "Poor dearest! He is so dreadfully prone to the hiccups. I shall just run and fetch him a bit of damson jam, for he cannot take the whole ones in his mouth."

"Can you not simply ring for a servant, Louisa?"

As she fled from the room, she threw an answer over her shoulder, not bothering to ensure that it made any sense. "Of course, but I must have a talk."

Instead of heading for the kitchen, Louisa tiptoed to

149

the front door. The footman, startled by her hushing gestures, quietly opened it for her. She did not go outside, but instead took a good look at the boy standing out in the street with the reins of Ned's horses in his hands.

With a silent thrill of satisfaction, she admitted that her audacious plan just might work.

She then made a trip to the kitchen, returning to the drawing room with a tiny spoon and a silver pot of jam.

Ned shook his head at her, a puzzled smile on his lips. "You needn't have rushed off so suddenly. His hiccups cleared themselves."

"They often do," she said, laughing at herself, "but it is so distressing when the poor love's body is racked. Well, I shall put this aside in case we need it later."

As she set it on the table, Ned stood with the baby. His grave expression told her he was about to leave.

"Oh, must you go?"

"I must. I simply wanted to pay my respects. You will take care of Little Ned?" His tone informed her he did not expect to see Robert Edward for some time.

"Of course, but we shall expect to see you the moment you return to London."

Ned made no response as he transferred the baby onto her lap.

"Shall I send any message to Christina?"

Although she had said this in her most casual voice, Ned's hands gave a jerk.

"No—that is, yes, of course. You must send her my compliments and my—my most earnest wishes for a successful completion of the Season."

Louisa couldn't bear to probe any further. "I shall give her your regards. She will be so unhappy to have missed your visit, but Robert insisted she drive out with him this afternoon."

A hard, cold smile etched its way across his face. "What a pity," he said.

"Isn't it?" For once, Louisa allowed all her sympathy to show. "I cannot help feeling that something has occurred to make Christina wretchedly unhappy, though she tries not to show it."

"You must not trouble yourself. She is young, and the young have foolish notions. She will get over it, whatever it is."

"I do not think so."

Ned refused to be drawn into a debate. He shook his head as if to rid himself of a worrisome pest. "Good-bye, Louisa. Be glad I have done something right for once."

He strode from the room without his customary good-byes for "Little Ned."

When Christina returned from her drive with Robert, she found her sister-in-law alone in the drawing room, sitting on a low divan with a handkerchief pressed to her forehead.

"Louisa?"

At the sound of Christina's solicitude, Louisa jumped and turned away. She gave the impression of wiping surreptitious tears from her face, before swiveling to greet Christina with a tremulous smile.

"There you are, my dear," she said with an artificially perky air. "How was your outing?"

"Louisa, is something wrong?"

"No, no, dear. It is nothing." Louisa craned her neck to look past her at the door. "Is Robert with you?"

"No, he let me out. He said he had some errands in St. James." Christina pulled off her bonnet while she searched Louisa's face.

Her sister-in-law was plainly trying to hide distressed

feelings. She refused to meet Christina's gaze, and all desire for speech seemed temporarily to have left her.

Christina moved to the divan to lower herself beside Louisa.

"You must tell me what has made you so miserable," she said, taking Louisa's hand to stroke. "It is not the baby?"

A startled sigh broke from her. "No, dearest, no, it is not the baby. If it were, I should tell you instantly."

"What then?"

"It is something you cannot know."

"Robert? Do not tell me he has been a brute?"

A laugh, quickly smothered, escaped from Louisa's lips. She covered them with her handkerchief as if to tamp down hysteria. "No, no! You must never think such a thing of your brother!"

"If you do not tell me what it is, my imagination will do far worse."

Louisa turned wide, fearful eyes upon her. "Oh, dear. I fear you are right. Although there could not be much worse."

"Louisa, you are alarming me!"

Louisa patted the hand that held hers. "Yes, I'm afraid I am. But, you see, you caught me just after his visit, and I was not prepared."

"His? Not Ned's?" Alarm clogged Christina's throat. "He is not hurt?"

"No, but he will be soon! Oh, how I wish Robert had not so gravely misunderstood the situation between you two! It was purely innocent. And poor Ned has borne the blame for something he did not deserve. His self-regard has taken such a blow, I fear it will send him back to his old ways."

"Why should you fear that?" Now that she knew he

had not been injured, Christina's pulse had quieted, but she was keen to know everything he had said.

Louisa slanted her a look full of guilt. "This is the part I should not tell you," she said.

"But you must!" Afraid that she might have betrayed too much feeling, Christina modulated her speech. "That is, you must not be afraid of wounding my sensibilities. I am not so fragile as you think."

Louisa hesitated, then nodded. "I have often thought it wrong to keep girls too much in the dark. We keep them packed in lamb's wool and then send them out to be married, completely unprepared for what they have to face."

"Yes, yes, dearest." Christina tried to hide her impatience, but she could not permit Louisa to become sidetracked by one of her causes. "But what did Ned say?"

"He said he was leaving London for a journey into Yorkshire. He did not know when he would return."

Although the knowledge that Ned was leaving caused a painful stab to her chest, Christina frowned. "This is what has you so overturned?"

"Yes! For you cannot imagine the wickedness he intends to get up to! It is always the same when he retreats into the country.

"Drunkenness and orgy! I have heard it whispered many a time. And Ned, although he tries to hide such things from me, betrays his guilt with his looks. He could scarcely meet my eye this afternoon."

"Oh." Now, Christina was truly alarmed, but even more dismayed by the feeling of helplessness that assailed her.

"Yes, *oh*. And I see nothing we can do to stop him. I can only hope one of his friends might. I had such hopes for Ned after the changes in him this Season. He had begun to look so sound. Now, because of a silly misunderstanding, all of that is lost."

"Do you think anyone will try to stop him?"

Louisa shook her head sadly. "I doubt he has the kind of friends who would. I tried, but he insisted he must be gone. It's as if he is running away from something that frightens him here."

A spark of excitement lit a fire in Christina's veins. What could Ned be running away from if not herself? She had thought she'd seen the light of love in his eyes when he had held her in her room. Only her fear of being wrong and the pain that would result if she exposed herself foolishly had kept her from pressing for an answer. Ned's present behavior seemed to confirm her dearest hopes.

Hadn't she sensed that Ned felt his youth was over? And had he not done his level best to guard hers? From what she'd observed, he seemed so sure he was not deserving of marriage or children, no matter how much he longed for the latter at least.

Had he removed himself from London to protect himself from her? Or her from him?

She could not let him go, if his going would confirm his worst notions about himself. But how to stop him?

Louisa had been searching her face, but she left off when Christina deliberately relaxed her frown.

"It is certainly too bad," Christina said, reining in her feelings.

"Yes, isn't it? And just when Ned has shown how truly noble and generous he can be."

"Oh?"

"Yes, he was telling me how he had saved a boy from the direst poverty by making him his new tiger. Of course, he was much more modest than I make him sound. But, whatever he said, I could tell he had truly exerted himself for a boy who had no claim upon him at all.

"And now I fear the poor boy will be corrupted, too!" Louisa buried her face in her handkerchief. Her shoulders shook.

Christina put an arm about her and hugged. "Is he going with Ned then?"

"Yes." Louisa spoke clearly in spite of her handkerchief. "The boy will ride behind him on his curricle into Yorkshire." She raised her head. "Oh, Christina, if you could have seen this boy. He is almost a man of course. But so innocent looking!

"He has rather long blond hair, although he wears a brown cap that hides most of it. I glimpsed him when I walked with Ned to the door. He looked so young in his rough black jacket and his baggy, black unmentionables, for he is scarcely taller than you. He's just a boy, merely a boy.

"And to think," Louisa continued on a wail, "that he will be riding all the way to Yorkshire alone with Ned, unaware of the ruin that will face him, but all too ready to grasp at the experience!"

"Oh?" Confusion made Christina frown again. "How can you know?"

Louisa sighed. "Ned said something about him before he left, which made me realize how particularly harmful an evil influence will be upon this boy just now. *He said*," Louisa stressed, looking Christina squarely in the eye, "that the boy is easily distracted from his duties by women."

A spark of an idea was born in Christina's mind. "He is, you say?"

"Yes. Is it not deplorable?"

"Of course. But he is of that age, I suppose, and as you say, if he has had a neglectful upbringing . . ."

"Precisely. It would not surprise me, if Ned were to come out of his house and find his horses gone one day.

"However"—surprising Christina, Louisa stood abruptly—"I have given both Ned and his tiger all the thought I can give without falling into despair. There is nothing more I can do. If Ned and his servant are to be saved from their own folly, it shall have to be at someone else's hands."

Christina had stayed seated while dangerous thoughts spun like a whirlwind in her brain. She scarcely heard Louisa as she departed the room.

Chapter Ten

$\mathcal{T}$wo o'clock on the following day found Christina standing in front of Ned's house, clad in a rough black jacket and breeches, with her hair tucked up under a brown knitted cap and the lower half of her face concealed by a course woolen stock. She held on for dear life to his spirited pair as she waited for Ned to come outside.

It had taken all her many resources to act so quickly, but she was both practiced and adept at this sort of masquerade. All she had needed was her maid's cooperation to make it work. But in spite of her loyalty, Mary had taken some persuading before she had at last agreed to her part in the scheme.

Fortunately, Ned had never been so affected as to dress his groom in livery. Under the strictest vow of secrecy, Mary had purchased the serving clothes and cap, along with a stout pair of shoes, and had smuggled them into the house. Then she had dressed herself in one of Christina's gowns in order to lure Ned's groom away from his stable.

Christina had asked Louisa for permission to spend the afternoon with an old schoolmate. This granted, she and Mary had left the house on foot, with Mary's dress covered by a cloak and Christina's boy's togs carefully concealed under her pelisse.

It had taken Christina no longer than a few seconds to

remove her pelisse and her stockings, which had been gartered at the knees, to roll her breeches down, and to substitute the shoes in Mary's parcel for her slippers. Her only concern had been for Mary's safety, but Mary had assured her with a toss of her brown curls that she had dealt with men more wearisome than this boy could possibly be. In any event, the timing had been so close, Christina had been forced to leave these concerns behind. She had only had a few seconds to slip into the stables before the call for Ned's horses had come from the house.

Now she would have a good three hours at least before the need to return home, which ought to give her plenty of time to accomplish her mission. She only need wait until Ned had passed the last house in London before revealing herself, at which moment she would do whatever she must to deter him from his present course of ruin.

She was counting on the traffic in the streets to occupy his attention, so that conversation between servant and master would be unlikely. Even if Ned discovered her before they left London, her appearance in these clothes would force him to be discreet. One way or the other, she would have a chance to talk some sense into his head.

The horses picked up on her nervousness. They plunged and snorted. For once, doubting her ability to hold them, Christina was struck with the enormity of what she had done.

The possibility of being exposed in the street nearly crushed her. What Ned would think when he discovered her playing at groom, she could scarcely bear to think. He would surely consider her as queer as Dick's hatband, like Caroline Lamb, who had disguised herself as a page to be near Lord Byron.

The sound of his front door opening made her jump.

Already frisky, the horses leapt forward. The tiny curricle, which had been built light for speed, served as no hindrance to their charge.

Nearly carried away, Christina hung on the reins with all her weight to resist the bays and managed to bring them to a halt after only a few feet.

"Hang on to them, Jem! There's a boy." She heard Ned's voice several yards behind her.

She tried to keep her chin down, for the stock around her neck tended to slip.

"Steady on." Ned spoke soothingly to his team as he climbed up onto the seat. "Ready to be off, are they? Well"—this last he added under his breath—"not half so ready as I. Stand away, Jem!"

Christina had been so distracted by Ned's previous phrase, she forgot who she was supposed to be until he called out impatiently, "Wake up, boy!"

She dropped her grip on the harness and ran around to the back of the curricle.

"Step lively now! You're running like a girl!"

Startled, Christina barely made it onto her perch in time. She had planted only one knee before Ned loosened his reins. The yank of the horses' forward leap nearly pulled her arms out of their sockets. It took all her strength to drag herself up onto the seat.

She had never realized how much the cushioning of a well-sprung carriage protected one from a bone-rattling ride. Her eyes wide as saucers, she held on with a tightened grip, fearing every second that the next loose stone or swerving turn would dislodge it.

Preoccupied with staying on, she did not notice at first that Ned was traveling south and east along the Mayfair streets. When she finally did, she became worried about his destination, until she persuaded herself that he merely meant to run an errand before heading out. It should be no matter. She still had plenty of time to return home with Robert none the wiser.

She felt the carriage slow and took the opportunity to peer around.

Ned had pulled his team to a stop in front of a block of houses. Not a shop was in sight.

Christina experienced her first jolt of anxiety. Until this moment, she had never suspected that he might be going to take on a passenger. Louisa had suggested he was heading into the country alone. But then, Louisa had had no notion of the mischief that would enter her sister-in-law's head.

The idea that his passenger might be a woman drained the blood from Christina's face. She suppressed a gasp.

How could she reveal herself to Ned in the presence of a woman? Worse yet, what conversation would she have to endure as she rode unnoticed behind them?

She had no time to ponder this, however, for Ned issued a sharp command to "Jem." She scrambled down, none too gracefully, and ran to the horses' heads.

"You needn't walk them." Ned jumped down and strode quickly toward the front door. "Not unless he keeps me waiting."

Christina was trembling now. Not only had the unaccustomed work been a challenge to her strength, but terror had gnawed a pit in her stomach.

"*He.* Ned said 'he.' " She repeated this word to herself for comfort. "His guest is a he."

Too late she realized that she could no more reveal herself in front of another man than she could a woman. Ned was already halfway to the door. Christina considered bolting, but if she did Ned's horses would bolt, too.

He might forgive her for an embarrassing prank, but he would *never* forgive her for endangering his horses.

Pluckily she held on, praying for another opportunity

of escaping before they were far outside London. She had a few coins tucked into her pocket in case of emergency. She could always use those to secure a ride. The only difficulty would be to find the opportunity before they got so far from London she could not return in time.

In less than two minutes, Ned reappeared at the door. Before she took a peek at his guest, Christina pulled her stock up about her mouth.

It muffled her squeak. Behind Ned she spied Levington strolling suavely toward the vehicle.

Behind him was a servant, carrying a small portmanteau.

"Throw it up behind," Ned instructed the man. "My tiger can hold on to it. My valet will come by later with the coach to collect his lordship's other boxes."

"Yes, my lord."

While this exchange was going on, Christina's mind whirled in torment.

Levington? Ned had invited Levington to accompany him on this trip?

She averted her face as much as possible and tried to raise the woolen stock about her mouth without letting go of the horses. But the two objectives were incompatible. Every time she ventured to let go of the reins, a horse would jerk its head.

"Hold them tightly now!" Ned warned, starting to come around to assist her. "Is something wrong?" he asked.

"Nothing, sir!" Even though he was standing far away, Christina could imagine the feel of his breath on her neck. She made her voice as low and gruff as she could. "I've got 'em right and tight now, milord."

Luckily, that stopped him before he got any nearer.

"Very well. But let me know if they're too much for you today. Sounds like you're taking a cold."

Christina would have laughed if she were not fully

conscious of being in a terrible fix. For once, she was certain she had gone too far and risked too much. Her only hope was the chance that she could slip quietly away before either gentleman suspected her identity, but she feared that such an occasion would be hard to find.

Ned got into his vehicle, took up the reins again, and gave her the word.

More sprightly now—inspired by a surge of panic— she sprang up onto the tiny seat behind him, which she now had to share with Levington's bag.

At least it afforded her an excuse to hunch her shoulders, which gave her some relief, although nothing could materially relieve her of an impending sense of doom.

The horses made the curricle lurch before settling down into a modest trot. With two men on board—and one terrified groom—Ned could hardly spring his team as he threaded his way through Town toward the Great North Road. Even at a reduced pace, however, they soon left London behind, and Christina found to her dismay that she could hear the two men's conversation far too well for her own comfort.

At first the two discussed Ned's curricle and team as well as sporting news about Town, but before long an awkward silence fell between them.

It was broken by Levington. "Although your hospitality comes at a convenient time, I must admit I was surprised by an invitation to Windermere Hall. I fail to see the purpose behind it."

"Why?" Ned appeared disinclined to be as frank. "You have been hunting with me there before."

"Yes, but that was before we exchanged rather heated words on more than one occasion, concerning a certain lady."

Christina could almost feel Ned's shrug behind her, although their shoulders did not touch.

"I see no reason," he said, "to carry on with animosity when the matter was so easily settled."

"Easily for you, perhaps. But not for me."

"Indeed?" Although he responded in an indifferent voice, fixing his gaze upon the horses ears' in front of him, Ned found it hard to resist the temptation to search Levington's face. He could not allow Levington to think that his answer carried any importance. But Ned felt a profound desire to know just how Levington's attempts to woo Christina had ended.

"Yes," his passenger continued. "I am afraid I wasted the better part of three months in pursuit of the lady."

"Wasted? She would not have you, then?"

"No. I have to wonder whether she ever had the slightest inclination to do so."

"When did this disappointment come about?"

Levington gave a bitter laugh. "At milady's ball, if you please. She had conferred upon me the honor of taking her into supper, so you will concede that my expectations were not unfounded. Then, calmly as you please, between the lobster patties and the pastries, she gave me my *congé*."

"Ahhhhh."

On this long, drawn-out note, Ned finally understood that he had made a fool of himself following Christina up to her room. Why had she not acknowledged to him then and there that her flirtation with Levington was over?

"You needn't sound so satisfied. Not unless you mean to have a go at her yourself."

"I?" Ned forced a look of surprise. "No. I'm of no mind to get m'self shackled. And even if I was, I should be no more acceptable as a suitor than you."

"With the lady or her guardians?" Levington's long look quizzed him. "The thought *has* occurred to me that the only reason Lady Christina could have had for playing me along as she did was to make another gentleman jealous."

A tightness gripped Ned's chest and throat. He responded shortly, "I assure you it could not have been me."

"I'm not saying you were interested. You have no need of her fortune after all, and I assume you have women enough. I only thought the lady herself might have had ideas."

"Not a chance of it. She must know she deserves a better fate than me."

His tone grown curt, Ned searched quickly for a different topic to remove Christina's name from Levington's tongue. He found only one. A dogfight was scheduled for that very afternoon along their route. He'd had no intention of attending it, but given Levington's obsession with wagering, a fight would be the very thing to divert his attention.

When Christina heard their talk turn to sports, she ignored their conversation. The names that floated to her over the rattle of the carriage—names like Spotty Sam and the Gripper, both likely to be pugilists—held no interest for her at all.

What *had* meant much were Ned's words on the subject of her merit. They lingered in her heart like a wealth of bright, glowing embers. His gentlemanly speech had inspired a warmth of gratitude that nearly made her turn about in the seat. Who better than he knew how little she deserved? And yet he had defended her. He had also adroitly turned the conversation to something else.

Christina could not indulge in speculation now, however, without the risk of revealing herself. All together, she must hold on to Levington's valise, the bouncing carriage, and her slipping cap, with only two hands to do the job of three.

What conscious thought remained, she turned exclusively on the question of how to get back undetected. So far, neither gentleman had evinced a need to stop, and a halt for the night was unlikely for a couple of hours, maybe more. If something did not happen soon to provide her with an answer to her dilemma, she would never get home in time.

She wished she could simply slip off the back of the curricle unnoticed. But once outside the metropolis, Ned had picked up his pace, and if she wrenched an ankle jumping off, her discovery would be certain.

Resigned to seeing this escapade through, whatever the cost, she gave herself over to the bumpy ride.

And bumpy it was. No matter how fine a vehicle Ned's curricle was, Christina was tossed and bumped about by the seat over every rut and stone.

Her head had begun to ache. Every muscle in her body hurt. And, from facing backward, she had evolved a rather pressing need to be sick. It was not long before Christina had to employ all her wits merely to keep from casting up her accounts. Consequently, the gentlemen's voices came to her as no more than an annoying murmur.

Finally, after an hour, they stopped to make an inquiry at an inn. Christina hopped down and stumbled to the horses' heads, grateful for any respite that would keep her off that seat. Hiding her face here was no problem, for her unsettled stomach forced her to rest her forehead against one of the bays' necks.

She had hoped to be relieved of this duty by an ostler, so she could make her getaway, but none came to help. They were busy with an inordinate amount of traffic. The yard was teeming with all sorts of vehicles, most of the sporting kind, as if every London buck had found Newmarket here in this small country town.

Her rest lasted no more than a few seconds before Ned and Levington were back.

As Christina threw herself back onto the seat, she must have launched a breeze Ned's way, for she heard him sniff.

He sniffed again. With prickles rising on her spine, she swore she could feel his breath on the hair of her neck.

She tried to bury that flesh between her shoulders.

Before giving rein to his horses, he half-turned around and asked, "Have you been washing, Jem?"

His direct question, this close, made her clutch at her seat. She muffled her voice. "Washing, sir? Me?"

"Yes, I thought I detected a whiff of perfume. Must be your soap."

Christina rolled her eyes to the heavens. "Oh, that, your lordship. Yes."

She felt him turn back around as he clucked to his team. "Out to impress the girls?" he asked. "Just make sure you don't forget your duties in the meantime." A puzzled note had entered his voice, which was unaccustomedly severe.

"I won't, your lordship."

At this rate, Christina thought, a sense of nervous desperation making her stomach toss, *I shall be discovered long before dark.*

The day was waning, though. Already, she had been gone much too long, and much too far in one direction to make it home before five o'clock. Whatever the outcome of this evening, she would have serious explanations to make, even grave charges to refute.

She rode in silence, grasping Levington's bag with a sense of grim fatality building slowly into despair. She had never meant for this to happen. No matter how wild she had been, she had never truly meant to be discovered in any of her peccadilloes. Deep down in her heart, she had not wanted to flout Robert's authority or injure Louisa's trust. She had only wanted to think poorly of herself so that the inevitable criticisms of others would not harm her so.

But her fear of the general censure that would result from this escapade was almost more than she could bear. Her guilt was so extreme it almost overrode her discomfort.

Just when she was certain her upturned stomach would force a confession from her lips, she heard Levington say, "We should turn in here."

Ned smoothly negotiated the corner of the main highway onto a private drive. In spite of his skill, the curricle lurched along the badly rutted road, exacerbating the headache that accompanied Christina's nausea. Mercifully, the drive was short. Only a few more yards led them to a spot where, peering around, Christina saw an isolated barn in the middle of a dormant field of maize, in which scores of vehicles had been stopped. Her gaze took in every kind of conveyance from gigs to handsome traveling coaches.

Grooms had unhitched many of the teams from their carriages to parade them around. Others simply stood at the horses' heads. Country boys, dressed in rough, rural garb, mixed with their city equals, some weaving their way through the crowd to offer their services to any gentleman arriving without a servant of his own.

This would be the fight they were talking about, Christina thought numbly.

Although she had never been to anything vaguely resembling a pugilistic match, she knew such matches were both common and illegal. Small wonder that two rakes like Levington and Ned would begin their orgy by observing one.

She had no doubt they would bet on the outcome, as

nearly all Englishmen did. Then, as she realized how many elegant equipages were there, she could only pray she would not be recognized by one of their gentlemen owners.

As soon as the curricle stopped, she jumped down, having no doubt of being required to hold Ned's horses and hoping she would find the strength. She was surprised, therefore, when Ned signaled to one of the local boys to take the reins.

"You, Jem," Ned called. "You may watch the fight if you wish. We've got a long journey ahead of us, and you will need the rest.

"Here"—as Christina kept her gaze downcast, hiding her face with the top of her cap, Ned reached inside his buff waistcoat pocket—"use this to wager with if you like."

He flipped a coin in her direction. Unprepared and still dizzy, Christina fumbled for it. It landed at her feet. Fighting the urge to dart a nervous glance up at Ned, she instead kept her eyes to the ground.

"Thank you, sir."

Ned lingered. She could feel his searching gaze on the top of her bulky cap.

"Are you perfectly well, Jem?" Uncertainty tinged Ned's voice.

With a worried beat thumping loudly in her ears, Christina muttered, "Yes, very well, sir. Thank you, sir."

Another brief pause, and he said, "Good lad. His lordship and I will only be stopping a few minutes. Don't lose sight of us, mind."

"No, sir."

As he finally walked away, Christina looked about her to determine what she should do. This could be her chance to escape. Indeed, it would be her only chance before nightfall, at which time the gentlemen would surely stop at an inn. She could not imagine the accommodations for a groom, but she assumed they would be neither comfortable nor private. A vision of the company she would be expected to bed herself down with nearly caused her to flee at once.

A moment's reflection, however, made her reconsider. It would be simpler to escape both Ned's and Levington's notice after dark. Easier, too, to rent a horse or other conveyance from an inn, when armed with a plausible story and a few large coins.

From this farm, she could travel only on foot, which would give Ned the clear advantage once he noticed his servant's absence and set out to look for him. Even with a horse, she would need an hour's head start to evade his rapid team. Common sense and a glance at the sun, moving lower in the sky, told her Ned would have to break his journey soon.

Having decided to wait until that moment to make a dash, Christina knew her principal task would be to stay undetected. Better, then, to act as Ned would expect Jem to do, and go see the match.

Christina took hasty steps toward the barn. Cheers, whistles, and shouts flowed out of its doors. The prospect of witnessing an event strictly forbidden to females normally would have excited her interest, but it could do nothing to stem her growing worry for Ned.

If she escaped, as she must, she would fail to stop him from his foolish course of action. With Levington nearby—evidently chosen to accompany Ned on his journey to the devil—she could do nothing to prevent him unless the two men somehow became separated. At the moment, she could think of no way to make this happen, and her time had definitely run out. As much as she wanted to save Ned, she could not risk being caught in his company overnight. The result would be ruin for her, with its resulting misery for him.

Still sick from her ride, she reached the crowd spilling out the door, a frightening mixture of Town tulips, bulky Corinthians, and local farmers all packed inside a small, dark space.

Shorter than the men, Christina knew she would see nothing of the match unless she worked her way to the front.

Secure in her disguise, which had managed to fool both men who knew her quite well, she pushed and inched her way past the shouting, gesturing spectators. The sound of snarls and loud barks up ahead, a low-pitched growl and a sharp animal squeal confused her, but her mind was too preoccupied and her digestion too overset to reason them out. She only wondered vaguely that dogs should be so stimulated by a boxing match.

She should have expected the sight that met her eyes as soon as she reached the center of the barn. As she forced her way past a portly gentleman holding a smoking cigarillo, she found herself pressed against the sides of a pen. The eyes of all men present were avidly fixed on its occupants.

Two curs stood locked in vicious battle. A mongrel of sorts—short, broad, and strangely muscled—gripped the other dog by the throat. His long white teeth and bone-crushing jaw had a strangling hold on the other one's neck. Blood dripped from their muzzles and tattered ears. Crimson gashes dotted their flanks. A length of skin and muscle from the weaker dog had been ripped clear away, exposing a bone.

In that moment of shock, Christina heard a sickening snap.

Trapped by the crowded bodies all around her, her

nostrils filled with smoke, her stomach already heaving, Christina felt her insides revolt. She went weak at the knees.

Ned had lost all interest in the dogfight long before it had ever begun. Although he had attended his share of matches from childhood, he had never relished the sight of two animals ripping each other apart. Levington, however, had declared his keen desire to see the match and to place a bet on Spotty Sam, the unfortunate cur that had just lost its life, and as his host, Ned had been forced to stay.

He gave a snort for the idiocy of men like his guest. Nearly at *point non plus*, Levington still could not resist the opportunity to throw his money away.

Concern for his normally loquacious tiger soon turned Ned's thoughts. The boy's movements had been sluggish today, his shoulders beneath his jacket appearing thin and hunched. The gruffness in his voice had led Ned to believe him sickened by a cold, in which case a trip this strenuous could send him lower still.

Ned glanced about the barn for a glimpse of the boy. He had not taken a look at Jem's face to see if his nose was red or his cheeks either hollow or feverish. There would be little he could do for the boy until they reached an inn, but if Jem proved to be ill, he would have to be sent home.

As Ned's eyes roamed over the heads in front of him, he spied a number of his acquaintances and drinking cronies. Lord Pepperill and Adrienne Mounts were earnestly cheering the winner on. At the betting tables, where Levington tried desperately to recoup his losses, more of Ned's friends were placing bets on the next contenders.

The male half of London appeared to be here, taking a well-deserved break from Society balls. For the first time today, Ned experienced a sense of misgiving over the possibility of finding lodging for the night. Judging by the number of vehicles out in the field, every room within miles would already be spoken for. He ought to have foreseen such a problem, but his mind had been hampered by a dull ache emanating from his chest as he thought of Christina.

He could almost see her now, her pale, delicate features rimmed with shadows. And, in the carriage, for one dizzying moment, he thought he had sensed her perfume.

Taking himself up short, Ned banished these painful images from his brain. He searched the barn for his tiger and spotted a suit of coarse, black jersey and a bulky, brown cap wedged tightly against the pen.

Ned managed a grin. It had taken Jem no time to wriggle his way up to the front.

Then, something about the boy's posture made Ned stiffen. Jem's head flew back as his legs collapsed.

Ned caught a glimpse of fine, blond hair escaping from the cap, a pair of anguished blue eyes, and two porcelain cheeks.

His stomach gave a leap and lodged in his throat. Quick anger followed on his fear.

Looking around, he saw that no one had noticed Christina yet as, mouth covered, she struggled to find her feet.

Moving as rapidly as he could while still maintaining a careless air, Ned worked his way through the shifting, noisome crowd until he reached her side.

He gripped her arm, pulling her onto her feet until her startled eyes flew up. Instantly, they lit with relief.

Her patent joy on seeing him doused Ned's anger like a smothered flame. A wave of pure emotion buoyed the heavy burden from his chest. Beneath her boyish garb and her English-rose complexion, he saw the evidence of a heart both loving and brave.

He had never been so happy to see anyone in all his life.

Badly sickened by the death match in front of her, Christina listed heavily on his arm.

Ned lowered his lips to her ear. "May I suggest we remove ourselves from here?"

Chapter Eleven

*C*hristina leaned on him gratefully, though she tried
to hide her illness while they negotiated a path to the
door. Then, a slap of fresh air from outside threatened to
knock her flat.

Ned half dragged her to the edge of the field and
settled her on a stile. He remained standing, shielding her
identity from the spectators behind them.

Christina took several tremulous breaths, but her knees
still felt as weak as jelly and nausea reigned supreme. In
truth, she thought it would never be vanquished, not after
the sight of those curs.

"Ned, how could you?" she wailed, when she could
speak without fear of hiccuping.

He chuckled in response.

Glancing at him with reproach, she met a pair of
laughing eyes.

"I might have known," he said, "that my forbearance
to lecture you for this prank would be thus rewarded. May
I inquire what I have done to deserve a hair-combing?"

"How could you watch such a mean-spirited thing?"

"One might ask the same of you, I suppose, considering the lengths to which you've gone to gain admit-
tance to the match."

So, he thought she had waylaid his groom just to

watch an illegal dogfight. It seemed improbable, but she was ready to leap on the excuse.

"I did not know how beastly they were," she mumbled.

"But you must have known."

Ned was smiling down at her as if every word she said amused him. She knew she ought to feel glad that he had not treated her to a lecture or a vicious shake. But it was far more pleasant to act angry than to give in to her queasiness.

He glanced over his shoulder at the crowd of vehicles, then said, "May I suggest that we dispense with this discussion while I figure out what is to be done with you?"

Shame overcoming her, she could only nod.

"Shall I assume that Robert has no notion of your whereabouts?"

"Yes—but, Ned, everything has turned out wrong. I did not mean to travel with you this far, but once Levington joined us, there was nothing else I could do."

He gave a throaty laugh, before a serious thought brought a frown to his brow. "Yes, I can see you were in a fix. If I am to take you home, however, something will have to be done about Levington, and soon."

"Can you think of a way to get rid of him?"

"Of course. Meanwhile, I want you to stay right here. Keep that muffler over your face, and do not speak to anyone."

She muttered, "I'm not a complete simpleton, you know."

Cutting her a wry glance before he departed, he offered, "We can debate that at a later date. Meanwhile, you will do as I say? I have your word?"

Christina drew up her chin. "I have no choice."

"There's a good girl. I'll only be a few minutes."

As Christina watched him walk calmly toward the barn, she issued a sigh that was at once hopeless and full of contentment. Ned's tall, athletic figure quickly merged into the group of rowdy men, but she had no doubt he would soon return.

And she would have nothing to fear. From this moment on, everything would be all right. Well, perhaps not everything. But, at least, she had stopped Ned from ruining his life, and he did not seem to resent her for it at all. And no matter what Robert and Louisa did to her once she got back to London, for tonight she could be with Ned.

The sight of his face bent over hers in concern had been so welcome. His evident pleasure on seeing her had been like a poultice to her aching heart. Despite the scandal that faced her at home, she would not regret her impulsive act.

Muffled by the distance, barks and snarls continued to erupt from the barn, joined by equally savage noises from the men. Before long this gathering would have to disperse, for there would soon be no daylight to illuminate the fighting pen.

Christina had been certain that Ned could not emerge from the crowd without her seeing him; but she was surprised by the sight of his curricle coming toward her. She covered her mouth with the stock and lowered her chin to be sure, but the driver was Ned.

"Hop up," he said, bringing the curricle to a halt beside the stile. The horses looked refreshed and eager to be off.

As Christina scrambled to her feet, he said, "You will have to forgive my deplorable manners in not handing you up. But I think you will agree, it would look a bit odd if I made a fuss over a person presumed to be my tiger."

Christina threw him grimace, which he returned, before the sight of her slim ankles below her breeches seemed to capture his interest. His gaze faltered.

Up until now, Christina had moved about in her boy's garb without the slightest bit of self-awareness, but her feelings became quite different under Ned's scrutiny. An appreciative smile hovered at the corners of his mouth as he clucked to his horses.

A pregnant silence fell between them. Christina did not dare ask where they would be going, or more particularly where they would spend the night, which would soon be closing in. She trusted Ned to bring them out of this predicament, although she feared the consequences might be far greater than he liked.

For his part, Ned was fully aware of the failing light and the compromising situation, as well as the probable outcome of this night. Intending to spare Christina as much disgrace as possible, he focused first on getting her home. He eased his team out of the rutted track and up onto the main road. But, once there, he told her to hold on tightly while he urged his pair into a gallop.

He could not possibly get her back to London tonight. Nevertheless, they should put as much distance as they could between themselves and the men behind them before dark. The worst imaginable occurrence would be for one of those spectators to recognize the Lady Christina Lindsay.

His near euphoria on seeing the light in her eyes had quickly given way to worry. He didn't know what had brought her on such a mad escapade, but the result would be foregone.

She would be forced to marry him.

Once Robert discovered she had left Town in Ned's company and spent the night with him alone, she would have no choice.

Ned's heart gave a stunning leap, but his concern for Christina tamped it down. He thought he could make her a good husband. He would surely try.

But no young girl with her beauty and spirit should be tied to a burned-out rake like him.

Ned pressed his horses until the fading light made the road too hazardous. While they'd kept up a rapid pace, conversation had been impossible. Now, as he slowed his team to a more restful trot, he cast his gaze on the woman beside him.

Christina's eyes met his, and in their depths he read her embarrassment over what was to come. Still, she looked at him with all the trusting wonder of the little girl he so fondly remembered.

Ned could not be certain that he merited that trust.

He broke their gaze and, with an effort at casual speech, said, "We shall have to find a place to pass the night."

"Shall we go to an inn?"

He shook his head. "We'd be certain to run into someone we knew. It would be better to find ourselves a barn."

Out the corner of his eye, he thought he saw her shiver.

"Scared?"

His question seemed to surprise her. "Of course, I'm not. Your mentioning a barn made me think of those poor dogs."

"Ah."

"Why *did* you stop there, Ned? I hope you do not enjoy dogfights."

On another day, at another time, he might have teased her; but Christina needed his reassurance now. "I have never cared for dog matches, but Levington does. I only stopped so he could place a wager."

"What did you tell him?"

"Levington? Oh, that was easy. I concocted a yarn expressly designed to appeal to the tenderest spot in his heart. I told him a messenger had tracked me down from London to deliver some very important news. My great-aunt Bertha, if you please, is not expected to last the night, and if I want to be included in her will, I had better make haste.

"In that sort of situation, you know, Levington can be astonishingly sympathetic. He said he had an aunt in similar health, and he was daily hoping for her to expire."

Christina made a noise between a laugh and a snort. "But whatever did you do to get rid of him?"

"We had several acquaintances in the crowd. It did not take me long to find someone willing to take him up."

"Thank goodness!" She gave a sigh. "I am happy you were put to so little trouble on my account."

Ned did not mention that he had offered to pay Levington's expenses on a shooting jaunt Lord Pepperill had arranged.

They rode along behind the horses as the late spring day turned into twilight. A pleasant breeze whipped up, bringing with it the scent of freshly turned earth. Meadow flowers filled the air with their delicate fragrance, along with the sweetness of new grass. The cooling gusts ruffled the hair beneath their hats, giving Ned a feeling of freedom, but he reminded himself that it would later carry a chill. Even though Christina in her heavy black jacket was more warmly dressed than in her usual light muslin gowns, she would need decent shelter for the night.

As they tooled along the country road, Ned realized that, if not for the worry he knew Robert and Louisa were surely experiencing, he would be completely content.

He carefully avoided the taverns and inns on the London road. Then, shortly before dark, he noticed a tidy-looking farm only a short distance away. Turning down its curling drive between two hayfields, he stopped the horses several yards from the house and, passing the reins to Christina, told her to wait.

After a good quarter of an hour, during which dusk turned to night, he reappeared with a large basket in his arms.

"Hold this," he told her as he climbed back up.

Christina felt around inside the basket. It contained a pair of folded quilts, a rough pottery jug, and a cloth-wrapped parcel, which smelled like bread.

Ned repossessed himself of the ribbons and guided the horses a short way, through the opening in a low stone fence, then past a dark henhouse and pigsty to a vast, well-proportioned barn.

In the increasing blackness, Christina could barely see him as again he told her to wait. Despite the quickness in her pulse, she felt no alarm, simply a sense of great anticipation, a quivering deep within her belly, and a pleasant tightness in her throat. She took a deep breath to calm these tremblings and drew in the sweet, musky odor of hay.

The creaking of a large barn door and a striking of flint reached her ears. They were followed by a glow of light, which illuminated from within the outline of the barn.

Ned emerged and, with his body completely in shadow, approached the curricle. He held out both arms.

Christina dropped their provisions down to him, then descended with the assistance of his hand.

Inside, the barn was both airy and cozy, with last year's hay scattered across the floor. A pair of working horses occupied two stalls in the corner. They snorted and jerked their heads at the sudden intrusion. The lantern Ned had lit swung slightly from a hook suspended from a central beam. Its warming rays swept in and out of the corners.

Ned left Christina in charge of the food, while he

unhitched his horses and brought them inside for a rubbing down. They had already walked off their heat, so he permitted them to nibble at the feed and drink water from a bucket as he briskly stroked their legs with straw.

Christina spread one of the coverlets down on a broad expanse of hay. Then, she delved into the basket and found a large hunk of cheese, a good loaf of bread—and a knife for both—two plain mugs, and a brown jug of ale.

She had barely laid out this simple picnic when Ned joined her, throwing himself down on the quilt to face her, with his shoulders propped on one elbow.

"You appear to have found a generous farmer," she said, handing him a length of bread.

She could see he was trying not to grin as he shook his head. "It's amazing how generous men become when they are paid three times what their goods are worth."

"Oh," was all she could think to say.

"Yes. Yon farmer was inclined to believe there was something havey-cavey in the notion of a person of quality desiring his barn for the night. I told him what I thought was a plausible tale of a sporting event and no inn rooms available, but he preferred to think the worst. Fortunately, I did not give him my genuine name, or I fear my reputation would be even more blackened than it already is."

"But he does not know you have a lady with you!"

"No, that he doesn't. He thinks you are my groom." Ned's smile held a secret she did not think she should ask to have clarified.

Somehow, however, that smile raised a blush to her cheeks.

His teasing gaze shifted to the ale. He filled his mug and hers, before he said, "Would you now like to tell me what this prank was all about?"

Christina's throat closed up. She nearly choked on a

clump of cheese. She had given astonishingly little thought to what she would say, excusing herself with the notion that time had been so short. She had not had enough of it to form a story.

That left her with nothing but the truth.

She could not quite meet Ned's gaze.

"Louisa said you had been so overturned by Robert's accusations, which she knew as well as I to be in error, that she was afraid you would do something rash."

"Oh?"

"Yes, she was afraid you would go on a sort of rampage, as it were. Do dangerous things, I suppose. Things you might later regret."

"What sort of things did Louisa have in mind?"

Unmistakable humor buoyed Ned's voice. Christina peered through the lantern light to find him staring at her with his cheeks held taut, as if one more word from her would send him into a gale of laughter.

At the sight of his extreme amusement, mortification spurred her tongue.

"How am I supposed to know what things? Rakish things, I suppose!"

"You mean like saturnalian orgies, where the wine flows freely and bare-breasted nymphs dance on the tabletop?"

"Do you deny it?" She poked her chin into the air. "You were taking Levington along with you, too. Considering the number of times you have warned me of the evil to be associated with that gentleman, I find it strange that you would seek out his company if you did not have a similar entertainment in mind."

"Of course. And I am to thank Louisa for inspiring you to come along on our jaunt. Did she think you would wish to play a nymph?"

Indignation came bursting from her lips like a rising

head of steam. "I did not wish to be one of your nymphs! I meant to stop you from making such a cake of yourself! However, if you'd rather be an ass, you may simply leave me here. I am quite certain I can find my way back to London."

Ned laughed and laughed so hard he had to roll over on his back. Rising to her knees, Christina tried to maintain an air of offended dignity, but his laughter was too infectious. She could not help wishing she could touch his face and feel his deep, delicious humor spreading through her own body.

His reaction had to mean that Louisa had misjudged his intentions. Either that, or he found the notion of her stopping him vastly amusing.

"Was that not your intention, then?" she finally asked, sitting back on her heels to gaze down on him.

Ned stayed where he was in the hay with one arm crooked under his head. His eyes held a softer glow.

"No, I did not plan to go to the devil as you feared. But you would have stopped me? Why?"

Christina felt a lump that teased and tickled her throat, making it hard to talk. She quickly turned away. Her pulse was humming like a frenzied ocean wave.

"Then Louisa must have been mistaken." She ignored his question as she gathered up the cheese and untouched bread.

"Was she? I wonder. Still, I'm surprised to hear she sent you on such a dangerous mission."

Christina had been trying to pick up the knife, but the low, seductive note in Ned's voice made her fingers feel clumsy.

"Louisa did not send me," she said, her voice small.

There was a long silence, before Ned raised himself to one elbow again. She felt the pressure of his relentless gaze as he studied her face.

After a moment, she said, "Why are you staring at me so? Are you thinking what a mess I look?"

"No. I'm thinking how beautiful your skin is in the lantern light. Christina, come here," he said softly.

She swallowed. Putting down the knife she'd so foolishly gathered, she awkwardly crawled to sit near the place where his hand rested on the quilt.

"Look at me, Christina."

Slowly, she raised her lashes to meet his gaze.

Instead of the mocking humor she'd half expected to find, she saw a loving tenderness she had never seen in his eyes before.

Her lips parted on a sigh as Ned reached one hand to cup her face.

He brought her down onto the hay beside him and covered half her body with his own. He gently stroked her hair, watching each smooth, straight piece as it fell through his fingers.

His gaze drifted back across her features to caress her eyes and her lips. "You may yet prove to be my salvation," he murmured.

Christina welcomed his kiss with every fiber of her being. She purred as his lips met hers and his gentle hands moved over her. Alternately gathering her body for a deeper embrace and freeing his hand to run his fingers over her cheek, her head, her throat, and her eyelids, Ned made gentle love to her.

She wanted to drown in his affection, to lose herself in his rising need, to forget all that she had ever been and never would be again.

In him, she sensed a similar wonder. A bright, new beginning that could never be sullied by memories of his past. To her, his past meant nothing except for that moment long ago, when he had held her on his lap and whispered comfort into her ears, when he had taught her the meaning of kindness. And now she felt herself hurtling back into that memory as if a bird were flying her home, back to a time before her aching restlessness had ever begun.

"Christina." He breathed her name on an ecstatic moan.

It made her smile, and she stretched like a cat.

"Christina, my love, I have to get you back to London intact, but if you continue to move like that, it will be more difficult than I care to admit."

"Intact?" With a questioning tilt of her head, she sought his eyes.

"Yes. Undefiled."

His lopsided grin, and its accompanying rueful look, made her chuckle. With a disappointed sigh, she said, "If you insist."

He heaved a sigh, too, and she delighted in its unsteadiness. She would never doubt that their embrace had affected him as much as it had her.

Ned left her in the straw while he corked the ale they had barely touched and covered the remaining food. Then he stood and smothered the light.

After a moment, Christina felt him kneel down beside her and cover her with a quilt. He lay down a few inches away, but she quickly closed them, snuggling into his shoulder. Although he wrapped one arm about her, she felt him tense.

After a while, he cleared his throat, and she listened as he said, "You know what Robert will expect of us now?"

His choice of words brought her up short. With a sense of deflation, she said, "I suppose I do."

"And you would have no objection?"

His even asking made her wonder what objections had come into his mind. Fear of these, when she had been so certain he, like herself, had embraced the notion of marriage with joy, made her respond with her former wariness. "Must we go through with it? I had no intention of forcing you into marriage when I came."

His pat on the shoulder reassured her that, at least, he did not suspect her of that. "Nevertheless," he said, "we must pay the piper." He cleared his throat again. "I shall try to make a good husband, Christina."

The strain in his voice nearly broke her heart. What could it mean, but that, in spite of the passion they'd shared, the thought of being bound to her still gave him pause?

"I know you would," she said, endeavoring to conceal her hurt beneath a practical tone. "But, who knows? If no one but my family ever learns of this mishap, perhaps you will not be trapped."

"I can think of much worse things," he said, but his sober timbre revealed nothing of his feelings.

"I agree. But shouldn't we wait to see what happens tomorrow?"

"I suppose."

As Ned lay there that night, pondering the regrets Christina must harbor for having put herself in such a hapless situation, he felt her move away from his arm. A blast of cool air filled the spot she had occupied, chilling him to the bone.

Was he not to lie every night with Christina beside him as he'd begun to hope?

All, it seemed, would depend upon Robert and his opinion of Ned.

Chapter Twelve

*R*obert discovered Christina's absence when he and Louisa sat down to a late dinner. He had not complained about the hour, for the cook had been instructed to prepare his favorite roasted capons with a truffle sauce.

"Where is Christina?" he asked when, after a polite wait, she did not appear.

"I am not sure." Louisa nervously applied herself to the asparagus soup. "She asked to spend the afternoon with a friend she knew at school. I had expected her to be back before now, but Marston says there has been no sign of her."

Robert hitched his brows. "Have you sent a footman round to collect her?"

"No." Louisa glanced at him contritely. "I am greatly afraid that I have forgotten the name of the friend she went to see."

"Good God." He fell back against his chair. "Did you say she went alone?"

"No, of course not! She took her maid."

"But you must remember the chit's name!"

"I cannot."

"Well, think. Was it Jane—Marie—Henrietta?" He kept reciting names, growing more worried by the second.

Louisa had hoped to get through dinner before Robert began examining her or grew this agitated. She had

187

hoped the roasted capons would do the trick, but saw that was not to be.

To put a halt to this torture, she played her next card. "Perhaps Marston will remember where she said she was going."

Robert's frown spoke volumes. "I should have thought you would have questioned him before." In a tone of wearying patience, he added, "Let's have him come in."

Louisa rang for their majordomo. She knew from experience that any conversation with Marston would take more time than it ought, due to the exaggerated dignity of his speech.

Nevertheless, Robert's queries to his butler occupied no more than a quarter of an hour, still leaving the whole of the night ahead.

Marston could not remember the name of the young female the Lady Christina had gone to see; however, he could state that her ladyship's maid had returned just after five of the clock. She had taken a tray upstairs, leading Marston to suppose that His Grace's sister had made her way back into the house somehow without his knowledge.

"Perhaps she's in her room, then," Louisa said, smiling.

"And did not come down at the gong? If that is so," Robert huffed, "then she is being abominably rude not to have sent us word." He eyed the tempting capons Marston placed before him at Louisa's request, but he refused to be distracted.

"Let's have this maid of hers down, shall we?"

"Before we finish dinner? It will be quite ruined if we wait."

"Christina could very well be ruined if she proves to be missing!"

"Robert!" Louisa's shocked whisper, accompanied by a glance their servant's way, reminded him to be discreet.

"Very well, then," he grumbled, but she could see that nothing would appease him. "It can wait that long, I suppose."

They ate hurriedly, with Robert declining any port after dinner, before he insisted on calling Christina's maid down to the drawing room.

Mary met them there, the fright on her young, round face enough to confirm Robert's worst suspicions. In a trembling voice, she confessed that Lady Christina had undertaken a prank, that she had thought to be back long before dinner, but had never returned.

"What was the nature of this prank?" Robert's restraint was near to bursting.

Tearily, Mary informed him of Ned's tiger, the clothes she had procured for her mistress, and the last she had seen of her riding away on the back of Lord Windermere's curricle.

"Windermere?" Sinking into a chair, Robert clapped both hands over his eyes. "She is ruined! My sister is completely and irretrievably ruined."

"That will be all, thank you, Mary." Louisa shooed the girl out with an admonishment to keep her story to herself. Then, with a contriteness she did not have to fabricate, she hastened to her husband and took up his hand.

"Do not be distressed, my dearest. I am certain everything will turn out right."

"I told Ned to stay away from Christina, but he must have gone against my wishes. It is clear he persuaded her to run away with him."

"No, no!" Louisa cried. "I am sure you are wrong. You heard what Mary said. Ned knew nothing of Christina's intentions."

"But what could have possessed her to do such a way-ward thing?"

"Well, as to that . . ." Louisa knew it was time to take her portion of the blame. This was the moment she had been dreading. "I am terribly afraid that something I said might have put the notion into her head."

Robert dropped his hand from his eyes and, with a look of increasing wrath, raised them to scrutinize her face.

"Louisa, what have you done?"

"Oh, Robert. You mustn't look at me with such suspicion. If I said anything to lead Christina to ruin, I am most heartily sorry. But I cannot believe it will come to that."

"It has already come to that."

"Now, Robert. I honestly think he loves her, and if that is so, surely he will do nothing to harm her."

"Ned, in love with my sister? Or anyone? He doesn't know the meaning of the word."

"I do think he loves her. And she, him!"

"Then she must be ruined. Have they gone to Gretna Green? Or is it something worse?"

A look of hope crossed Louisa's face. "Oh, do you think they might have gone to Gretna? That would account for her being so late! I had not thought of that."

Robert gave a snort of disgust. "Yes, I suppose we must hope he has taken her to Gretna and not simply ravished her instead. But you have not yet told me what you said to make her go off on such a start."

Recalled to her own crimes, Louisa winced. "I merely told her that Ned had been here and that I was afraid his disappointment would drive him back into his old ways. Which was true! I have been afraid he might eventually drink himself to death or break his neck in a carriage race if he does not settle down."

"You must have said more than that."

"Well, perhaps she thought I meant he was in immediate danger. Which he might have been, which is probably why she went to save him now."

"Louisa, surely Ned told you he was taking Levington on a shooting trip."

Louisa felt the color draining from her cheeks. Her fingers flew to her mouth. "Levington was to go along? Oh, dear! I quite see now why Christina did not come back after speaking to Ned."

"Do you? Then you have a sharper mind than I." Robert stood abruptly and started for the door. "I shall have to track them down."

"But Robert"—Louisa ran after him and took his arm—"how can you leave when we don't know where they've gone? They could be anywhere between here and Scotland."

He looked down at her impatiently. "Do you expect me to do nothing?"

"No, but first we must give them a chance to return. They may be on their way back right now. Surely, if Christina's intention had been to go to Scotland, she would have left us a note."

Robert raked a hand roughly through his fair hair. He was clearly muddled as to the course he should take. "I could travel up to Ned's estate. See if they've stopped there."

"I cannot believe they have gone so far, but perhaps Ned did not discover her until they were far outside London. In that case, he might have taken her up into Yorkshire, although I am inclined to think he will bring her back just as soon as he can."

"That's what an honorable person would do," Robert said with doubt.

"Then we must put our faith in Ned."

"Faith in Ned! Have you lost your mind completely, Louisa?"

She drew herself up and dropped her hold on his sleeve. Her eyes filled with moisture.

"There, there," Robert said, patting her shoulder awkwardly. "I did not mean to snap at you so, but all along I have wondered at your trust in those two. They have never merited it, and only see what has happened now."

Louisa made a great show of drying her eyes with a handkerchief. She was desperate, and tears were her only weapon left. And weeping came quite naturally, she found. Although she thought she knew both Ned and Christina well enough to guess how they would behave, she could not be absolutely certain that the girl was safe. Louisa *might* have inspired her sister-in-law's ruin, just as Robert said.

"I have to believe they will come back just as rapidly as they can. And if you rush out to look for them in the dark, you could pass them on the road."

"Very well." Robert's agreement was reluctantly given. "I shall wait until morning. But if they are not returned by a reasonable hour, I shall have no choice but to set up in pursuit."

"I shall mention to my dresser that Christina has stayed overnight with her friend. That should put a stop to any rumors belowstairs."

Louisa left him alone in order to do just that. Then, before she returned to the drawing room, she made a trip up to the nursery to see that Robert Edward was all right.

Christina's nephew, Ned's godchild, peacefully slept on his stomach, a little fist clutched tightly to either side of his head. When Louisa looked down at him, she was comforted by the thought that any two people who had discovered their desire for a baby should have the good sense to recognize their perfect mates.

The night was both difficult and long with Robert's pacing and despairing. His indecisive character made him chafe against the wait she'd imposed, and more than once Louisa had to reason with him again to keep him from rousing all his servants and setting out.

About dawn, he did rouse them, telling them to prepare for a quick journey north. Neither Robert nor Louisa had much appetite for breakfast. How could they eat when every clatter in the street or tradesman's call made them start?

After a long debate, they agreed that ten o'clock would be a proper time to give up on the miscreants and for Robert to begin his search. Every minute of the morning was like a punishment to Louisa for the risk she had taken with Christina's welfare.

By half past nine, Robert was dressed in his traveling clothes with cloak and gloves pulled on, pacing the drawing room with, Louisa thought, a quite unnecessary riding crop in one hand. As she waited, sitting anxiously on the couch, he repeatedly struck the whip against his boots with every step. A heavy scowl marred his normally sanguine features.

Another carriage rumbled out in the street. They had jumped at far too many to peer out again, but this one seemed to stop.

Louisa's eyes met Robert's as she rose to her feet.

A loud knock at the door, and Louisa reached for Robert's hand to prevent him from making a scene in the corridor.

They heard Ned's voice. "The lad is my tiger, Marston. I have need of him in the drawing room. Is your master about?"

"Yes, my lord. I believe His Grace and Her Grace are awaiting you."

Louisa grimaced at Robert. Their attempts at subterfuge had not been adequate to stifle the servants' gossip, but at least Ned had concealed Christina's identity.

A footman opened the door to reveal a wan, disheveled Ned, whose anxious face sported a full night's growth of beard. Behind him in the corridor stood what appeared to be a boy, his thin, huddled figure loosely clothed in black, his face partially covered by a large, brown cap and a woolen stock.

"This is the servant I spoke to you about, Louisa," Ned said with a sharp, direct look into her eyes. "I believe you expressed a desire to speak with him."

"Yes!" Louisa hurried forward. "Do bring him in! I am so glad you have come. And you see, you have caught Robert just in time, for he was about to journey north. But perhaps he will wait."

Once they were inside the room, she told Marston and the footman that they did not wish to be disturbed. Then she closed the door on the stony-faced servants.

Ned saw the lack of sleep on their faces, the signs of suppressed fury in Robert's eyes, and misery gripped his chest.

He turned to extend a supportive hand to Christina just as she shook the cap from her head.

Her blond, silky hair fell down onto her shoulders. She swept it out of her eyes.

Even as he faced the grimmest moment of his life, Ned could not help experiencing a feeling of pleasure at the sight.

"Christina, how could you?" Robert began in a scathing tone.

Ned instinctively sprang to her defense. "Wait right there, Robert. You must give her time to explain. Christina's intentions were decent. And what may appear to you to be an unpardonable sin was nothing more than a prank gone awry."

"I do not need you, of all people, to tell me how to address my sister, Ned. Her prank, as you call it, has led to her ruin, I make no doubt."

This last phrase, uttered with scorn, had the effect of prodding Ned's ire. Reminding himself of his own ghastly reputation, which he for so long had helped to cultivate, he strove to contain his temper. He could not let Robert believe the worst of Christina. Or of himself, if he wanted Robert's blessing.

"Nothing of a drastic nature has taken place, I assure you, and Christina will confirm what I have said. Nor has anyone but the four of us in this room any inkling that she passed the night in my company. Her reputation is safe."

Robert's jaw, which had been firmly squeezed, now opened incredulously. "So you would bring her back and ask us to pretend that nothing has occurred."

"Nothing *has* occurred!" Ned almost cursed at his friend's stupidity. "And, of course, I do not expect you to pretend. I have every intention of marrying Christina if you decide such a step is both desirable and right."

Christina flinched beneath his choice of phrase. Up until now, she had allowed the men to carry on. She had wondered how Ned would express himself upon the subject of their marriage.

They had spent the morning riding side by side in gloomy silence. Christina had not been certain how much of Ned's dread was due to the prospect of facing Robert and how much to the probability that he would be forced to wed her.

She had prepared herself to intervene. Now that she knew what his feelings were, she could stop this charade before it crushed her any further.

She opened her mouth to speak, but Robert, who had been pacing, had seized on Ned's words even more rapidly and he broke in, "You would marry her, you say, but there is no need? Christina, is this true?"

She nodded and tried again to speak.

But for a second time, Robert forestalled her. He seemed arrested by a thought. "You mean no one saw her? No one has any notion of this prank besides her maid?"

"No one," Ned said. His features were stony as he reported, "Once I discovered that she had ridden with me in place of my groom, I took pains to keep anyone from catching sight of her face. I left Levington behind with a fabricated story explaining why I had to get back to London. A farmer gave us shelter in his barn, but he believed her to be my groom."

Robert's gaze moved back and forth between them as if he detected their strain. "And nothing happened between you in the barn?"

Christina saw the muscle in Ned's tightened jaw give a twitch.

"I have said that I will marry Christina if you so wish. We have both made it clear there is no need. You may take it that nothing material occurred between us."

Nothing material? Only that she had found her heart and her peace, which he was doing his best to wrest from her now.

Robert resumed his pacing.

Christina distraughtly sought Louisa's gaze, in which she saw mirrored her own distress.

Robert came to a halt in front of his sister. "Then all is not lost. If no one is the wiser, I do not see a need for Christina to marry Ned at all."

"But Robert, surely—," Louisa began.

Christina turned to watch Ned's face, but the relief she

expected to see was not there. Instead, Ned stood frozen, his jaw locked with unexpressed grief. His eyelids flickered once, as if he'd been struck, before he schooled his features again into a tight emotionless mask.

"Christina, you will marry Lord Musgrove as soon as he comes up to scratch, and he need never know you were nearly compromised by the greatest scoundrel in London. You may count yourself fortunate indeed that this foolishness of yours has not wrecked your life.

"And as for you, Ned"—Robert turned back, and as if a cork had been loosed from a bottle, he spewed out all his pent-up wrath—"I know my sister would never have been so foolish except for your corrupting influence. That you have no regard for Society's rules is your own affair. That you would purposely set out to corrupt a young, innocent female, one moreover who belongs to a family with whom you have been intimate—"

Christina saw Ned standing at stiff attention like a vanquished soldier, bearing Robert's harsh accusations unflinchingly, and the sight of his precious features clenched against the pain made her desperate. She knew how unfair Robert's charges were. She also thought she knew how much each unjust phrase chipped away at Ned's heart.

She couldn't stand it any longer. She couldn't stand for Ned to take the blame for what she had done, or for anyone to hurt Ned.

She took the three short steps between herself and Robert. "That is enough! I say, stop it right this instant! I will not permit you to abuse Ned, when you must know how much he has done to try to save me from myself."

All eyes turned her way: Robert's, with shock; Louisa's, with relief. Even Ned had been jerked out of his stiffness.

"You have no idea," Christina continued, glaring at her brother, "how many times I nearly disgraced this family in some irreparable way. And each and every time, Ned was there to stop me from making a mistake he knew I would regret. He always came to rescue me. He is the only person who has ever understood me.

"And throughout these many months, he has acted with the purest, most selfless instincts of any man I have ever known. He is good and kind and noble, and he has proved the best of friends. And if he would have me for a wife—"

Christina faltered over these last words. They had cost her all her daring. But her courage did not fail her.

"—I should be the proudest and happiest woman alive."

She hardly dared to look up to see Ned's expression, but when she ventured a peek she saw a sight to gladden her heart.

His crooked smile, which had always drawn her with its fun, held so much more than mere amusement now. In his gaze, she saw a bright, sharp gleam of pride. And as she returned his stare, the gleam deepened and deepened into a glow, lightening her heart with every passing moment as it bade her to accept something more.

She felt his need of her, his desire to give her all she would ever require, and the same aching tenderness she had experienced at his hands last night and so very long ago.

"Christina—," Robert started.

Ned cut him off, his eyes never leaving her face. "Excuse me, Robert. I believe it is my turn to speak."

He moved to take up her hands, and the warmth from his started spreading through her.

Still speaking to Robert, though he directed his gaze to her, he began huskily, "Remember, Robert, when you said that all you desired in life was to see me humbled before a woman? Well, I am happy to give you that pleasure now."

He dropped to one knee and, looking up at Christina, he clutched both her hands to his chest. "I declare myself humbled before the Lady Christina Lindsay. I love her with all my heart and adore her with all my might."

His eyes were filled with the longing of love as he continued. "I never knew what it was to desire until I met her. I never knew what courage and loyalty could be until she showed me. I want nothing more than to make her happy, to give her a home, to father her children and watch them grow.

"I give you my word, Robert, that I will make a good husband to your sister. I know I am not worthy to clean her boots, but I shall never give you cause to doubt, and I shall love her and keep her till death us do part.

"And if my past still concerns you, I vow that no drop of wine shall cross my lips unless it is poured by her hand. Her fortune will remain her own, safe from me. And no other woman will ever share my bed or even my thoughts.

"All I beg is a chance to prove how much I will love her for the rest of our lives."

Christina's throat was so clogged with tears, she could only return Ned's gaze with watery eyes.

Louisa took noisy refuge behind a handkerchief.

It was left to Robert to respond, although he was so dumbstruck, he could scarcely turn words into speech.

"Well . . . ," he said. "Well, well, I must say. This puts a whole new face on the business. I am sorry, Ned, if I have accused you unjustly. I had no idea—I never thought that you, of all people—and Christina, for goodness sake! Well, I—"

"Robert," Louisa emerged from her handkerchief, "why do we not give Christina and Ned some privacy?"

He jerked, not a little embarrassed. "Yes—at least, I presume that would be all right—I suppose they are engaged, so it should not matter. We can sort out the legalities later. Send a notice to the *Times* and all that. That agree with you, Ned?"

Christina, still looking down into Ned's precious face, saw a glint of his old humor. His boyish, laughing eyes shone up at her.

"That will be perfectly fine, Bobby boy. And you have no need to worry about the proprieties. I have far too much respect for my affianced bride to seduce her in your drawing room."

"Oh, well—," Robert gave an embarrassed chuckle. "No need to be concerned anymore. What I mean to say is, engaged and all that. None of my business, really."

"Come, dear." Louisa took her husband by the arm and, beaming a smile back at the couple, pulled Robert away.

Christina could barely wait until the door closed behind them to run her hands through Ned's thick, ebony hair. She bent to plant a kiss upon his forehead, which served to bring him rapidly to his feet. He swept her into a suffocating embrace.

"Do you truly love me, then?" she asked, when her breathing had finally been restored.

"Not at all. I only live to please Robert."

Christina laughed, but a tender part of her needed to hear his declaration all over again in private. Her eyes made the plea.

"I do love you," Ned relented, speaking softly in her ear. "And I have for quite some time."

"Yet, you wouldn't tell me. Didn't you know I've been in love with you from childhood?"

"Is that why you tried to drive me frantic with your pranks?"

"Of course. I had to make you pay attention. How else could I capture a rogue as experienced as you?"

"I wanted you to catch me. God, how I wanted it! But I knew you deserved someone superior to me. The trouble was, I couldn't think of anyone who could do a better job of keeping you out of mischief than myself."

"Shall I promise you to stay out of trouble? Or would you suffer tediously with a tame sort of wife?"

"I will take you any way you want to be."

"Are you sure you won't be bored with a wife who adores you to distraction?"

"Not if it is you," Ned said seriously, drawing back to promise her with his eyes. "I meant what I said to Robert. I love you because you are beautiful and brave, yes, and bewitching and beguiling. But most of all, I need you. For you see something in me that others never have seen. When I am with you, I am no longer alone."

His words echoed so plainly with her own feelings, Christina felt no more need for questions now.

She offered up her face for his kisses, discovering in them all the tenderness she had missed most of her life. Her restless emptiness was gone; her long-overburdened heart felt full and light.

"This doesn't mean," Ned said later, when they had settled down to sit with Christina's head cradled on his chest and his arm held tightly around her, "that we need to conform completely to Society's mores."

"No?"

"No, I have wanted to flaunt one particular more at least. The one which says that husband and wife shall inhabit different rooms and sleep in different beds. I find that much too inhibiting for a rogue."

Christina relished the blush that infused her from her head to her toes. "As a fellow rogue, I do most heartily agree. We shall simply have to make our own set of rules with respect to those habits."

"How soon?"

"Have you no more patience, sir?"

"None at all. I've wasted enough of my life alone, without you."

"Then you have my permission to apply to my brother for a speedy wedding, as soon as the arrangements can be made."

Ned gathered her snugly in both his arms, and his voice was full of emotion as he said, "Then a fine pair of rogues we will be."